Scam a Bleeding Heart

Unpopular Opinions Book Series, Volume 4

Taseef Farook

Published by Unfiltered Ink, 2025.

Table of Contents

Yaad | Chapter 1. Fraud 1

Yaad | Chapter 2. Playing dress-up 19

Yaad | Chapter 3. Double standards 31

Nida | Chapter 4. Influencer 39

Nida | Chapter 5. Fairytale prince 59

Nida | Chapter 6. Live and let live 77

Nida | Chapter 7. Protests..95

Nida | Chapter 8. Happily never after... 109

Yaad | Epilogue... 123

Copyrights Page

SCAM A BLEEDING HEART

By Taseef Farook

The fourth part of the Unpopular Opinions Book Series

ISBN (paperback): 978-1-7638775-7-3

ISBN (Ebook): 978-1-7638775-6-6

Published by **Unfiltered Ink**

Adelaide, South Australia, 5000, Australia

Email: taseef@live.co.uk

Cover Design © 2025 by Taseef Farook

Unfiltered Ink is an imprint of Dr Farook Ink.

Dedication

To my mother, who has been scammed many times in her life!

Preface

Scams and fraud come in many forms, some so deeply embedded in society that they've become normalised, blending into the very flaws that plague our systems. My goal with this book was to bring the most prominent forms of fraud together into one cohesive narrative, continuing the theme of the *Unpopular Opinions Book Series*.

As with my previous books, while all characters in this story are entirely fictional, their struggles reflect real, systemic issues—problems that are often uncomfortable to confront. I believe humour and wit provide the best way to navigate such sensitive topics, making them more accessible without diminishing their importance.

This book marks my fourth attempt in the series at bringing these stories to life, inspired by the many people who have fallen victim to scams and societal prejudice. Once again, I am deeply grateful to my partner, Lameesa Ramees, and my good friend, Ragib Farhat Hasan, for their unwavering support in helping me complete this story. I couldn't have done it without you.

Blank page

SCAM A
BLEEDING HEART

Yaad | Chapter 1. Fraud

" *Rather fail with honour than succeed by fraud"* – Sophocles.

Last month, social media was flooded with news of my brother Beebo's death.

This week, the media erupted over a massive corruption scandal involving my brother-in-law, Kaushal Veni—right around the same time I received word that my sister, Nida, had stabbed Kaushal and was now in police custody.

If you immediately assumed she was defending herself from an abusive, corrupt husband and was wrongfully indicted, most people would probably agree with you. Most people I know wouldn't care to hear the details if the genders were reversed. But I want to approach this objectively—because the woman in question is my sister, and the man in question not only married her but also voluntarily took in our father and Beebo. Nida had always praised him for the way he cared for the family, giving her the "happily ever after" she had always dreamed of as a child.

Kaushal wasn't just another name in the news cycle though. He was a well-known corporate celebrity, serving as the Chief Overseer of the Turag Project—the country's least-discussed yet longest-running mega motorway initiative, which had been under development for thirty years. Locals called it a cursed project, as every Chief Overseer before him became a public figure overnight, only to either go insane or vanish off the face of the earth after inevitably failing to complete it within their tenure.

So why did he take it on? Because he had been obsessed with it for a long time, and Nida encouraged him to pursue it—despite knowing that no one before him had ever managed to get too far.

And more interestingly? He was the first Chief Overseer actually on track to finishing the project.

Until everything suddenly went south. Almost like a curse.

Let's go through exactly what happened.

It all started when they kicked Beebo out of their home, fearing for their daughter Samira's safety.

Actually, I should go back a bit further. Five years ago, Nida and Kaushal had a beautiful daughter—my niece, Samira. On the surface, Nida seemed to have the perfect little family, with everything going her way—except for whatever Beebo had done to get himself kicked out just a few months before my last visit.

But during that visit, something felt off. She didn't seem like herself, and no matter how much I tried to get her to open up, all she would say was that everything was under control and that I had nothing to worry about.

Like any concerned brother, I too pinned her strange behaviour on her husband. I asked her repeatedly, "Is Kaushal abusing you?"

She always gave the same response: "Kaushal is the least aggressive person I know. Even I'd be surprised if he ever laid a hand on me."

Logically, my sister deactivated all her social media profiles when Beebo's death flooded the internet. I knew how brutal online trolls could be toward the loved ones of the deceased. Before going offline, she sent me a message:

"I'm going offline to preserve my sanity. Don't worry, I'll message you when this all blows over."

She never came back online, which I assumed meant she and Kaushal had gone into hiding, anticipating the Kaushal Veni scandal before it broke in the media. It seemed like the perfect opportunity for scammers—posing as authorities, assuming false identities, and exploiting loved ones by preying on their fear of potential consequences.

So naturally, when the "Bangladesh police" contacted me, claiming Nida was in custody and needed bail, I was quite sceptical. I received a random WhatsApp call, followed by a message from an unknown number—first claiming to be Officer Oshim, and the next day,

Sergeant Alaul Mofiz. I instantly dismissed it as a scam. My brother-in-law was a well-known public figure in Bangladesh—if something had truly happened to him, it would have been all over the news. And considering he had just been caught up in a scandal, like most famous people eventually are, it seemed obvious that someone had seen his name trending and was now trying to use it to scam me out of money.

The message read:

"Your sister is in police custody. You need to bail her out by paying 4 lakh Bangladeshi taka."

It was followed by seven different forms demanding an absurd amount of personal information. Even if I had believed Oshim/Alaul was a real officer, it still reeked of a phishing scam designed to steal my money and identity.

After two days of persistent messages, I finally blocked the number.

The claims were ridiculous. One message said, "Nida stabbed Kaushal with a box cutter." Another said, "Nida fought back against Kaushal." None of it made sense. I was having a hard time believing it especially since it wasn't on the news and because I hadn't received an official letter from the police by email or post.

But then I realised something—Nida's phone was switched off. I couldn't reach her.

As much as I was 99% sure it was a scam, a small part of me hesitated. What if it wasn't?

I started thinking logically. Maybe, since I lived abroad, they didn't call me directly. It's not like local police stations in Bangladesh were rolling in money to make international calls. They relied on "unofficial donations" from bikers who refused to pay off the exorbitant fines for not wearing helmets, driving unregistered motorcycles, and blasting illegal exhausts loud enough to rupture eardrums—all while barely crawling by at five kilometres per hour. Ah yes, the pride of our community... *sarcasm fully intended.*

Then, finally—Nida's number rang. I picked up immediately.

"Finally! Where have you been?"

A tired voice spoke back. "Yaad. It's been two days—I'm in police custody. Please help me."

I froze. "Wait. That wasn't a scam?"

"No, it's true."

I was still trying to process it. "Wait... does that mean—Kaushal? Did you kill—?"

Nida hesitated, murmuring something under her breath, as if rehearsing her words. Then, with an exasperated sigh, she finally said,

"No, Kaushal's fine. I just... I had no choice. When he lunged at me, I had to defend myself—I had to stab him."

I cut straight to the point. "Where's Samira?"

Her voice softened. "She's with Kaushal's mother."

I understood the gravity of the situation but couldn't help the smirk forming on my face. "Did you try reaching out to the Colonel?"

A chuckle escaped her on the other end. "Oh, I called him too. The moment he heard I was in jail for stabbing my husband, the first thing he said was—"

I finished her sentence. "'This is a matter that should be dealt with within the family'?"

She laughed. "That is *exactly* what he said before hanging up. Then he stopped picking up my calls." Her laughter quickly turned to quiet weeping. "Yaad, I have no one. I'm so lonely here. Please get me out."

I tried to calm her down. "Okay, how do I pay for bail? Where do I transfer the money?"

"Transfer? You have to come in person to bail me out!"

I was baffled. "Nida, I'm over eight thousand kilometres away! And cash only? Are you in police custody or being held hostage? Blink twice if it's the latter!"

She let out a weak laugh through the phone. "There, I blinked twice. But seriously—please come."

I hesitated. "Nida, I... need to hear your side of the story first. You've been off the radar for quite a while, and now some Alaul Mofiz tells me you attacked Kaushal with a box cutter. And to make things worse, Beebo's story was all over social media last month, but I have no idea how he even ended up there!"

Nida didn't waver. "Beebo didn't try reaching out to you afterward?"

I replied quickly. "Not at all. The last time Beebo and I spoke was years ago—when he asked me for money, and I told him to get your permission first."

"Yeah, I remember. And you're right." Nida exhaled sharply. "Okay, just get here—I'll tell you everything."

I paused before asking bluntly, "Nida, be honest with me... did you have a good reason for what you did?"

She answered without delay, "I'm not crazy, Yaad. Yes..." she paused, "We...*I* had a good enough reason."

"Fair enough. See you soon!"

Just like that, I had to make the difficult call to my workplace to request emergency leave. Then, I dialled my partner, Lily. I told her everything Alaul and Nida had shared with me and explained that I'd be flying back to get my sister out of jail. She responded nonchalantly, "There's a lot of political unrest going on in Bangladesh right now, Yaad. Please be careful. And remember—start the negotiation with the police at half their asking price. You don't want to be *that* guy who pays the full 'asking bribe' at a police station!"

...

As I stood at the train station, ready to catch the train to the airport, I unblocked Alaul but couldn't shake the nagging feeling that Alaul might be trying to scam me, even after speaking to Nida.

I chalked it up to all the scam calls I'd gotten over the years—thick accents, broken English, and wild claims like being able to fix my love life if I just gave them remote access to my bank account. What irritated me most was how aggressive they'd get when I didn't buy their nonsense. That same pushy vibe was coming from Alaul after his third failed attempt at explaining the situation. But his messages were coherent and polite. The narrative wasn't his doing—it was Nida who committed the crime, and he was just reporting the facts. So why did it all feel so off? *Why was I not being able to trust a complete stranger asking me for money?*

As I was mulling it over, the answer quite literally walked up to me.

"Nice sunglasses," a stranger said as he approached.

That's when it clicked. In Australia, there's a breed of local, well-educated scammers who hang around train stations. They don't bother spreading the word of their God—which is annoying enough when unsolicited. Instead, they launch into a pitch about how they were once struggling international students until a mysterious business mentor taught them the "secrets" of entrepreneurship, making them wildly successful.

It always starts with a compliment—something trivial, like your sunglasses—before they ease into asking if you've ever considered leaving your stable job to "be your own boss." If only they were sincere and not trying to rope you into a pyramid scheme. The only ones who truly profit are the founders, who either end up in prison for financial fraud or flee the country, evading an international arrest warrant. Meanwhile, the victims who recognise the Ponzi scheme for what it is rarely complain—at least, not while they're still getting paid. It's only when the money stops that they suddenly become the victims.

"Thanks," I replied.

He immediately followed up, "Are you from around here, or were you an international student?"

"I was an international student years ago," I answered.

"So, what do you do for a living?" he asked, edging closer to his sales pitch.

"I'm a surgeon," I said, deliberately leaving out the details.

Without missing a beat, he switched to high gear, "Oh, you must have a lot of money saved up. Have you thought about starting a business?"

"No, and I'm not interested," I replied flatly.

But these in-person "pig butchering" scammers are relentless. He tried to sound relatable, "I was in your shoes once—an international student, unsure about my future until I met a mentor who taught me about entrepreneurship. Now, I'm a successful entrepreneur myself. You could be too!"

Thankfully, my train arrived. "Sorry, not interested," I said as I hopped on, thinking that was the end of it. But, of course, it wasn't.

He boarded the same train and rode halfway to the airport with me, blabbering nonstop about "entrepreneurship." Here's the thing: real entrepreneurs don't need to announce that they're building something big—their actions speak for them. These wannabes, on the other hand, love to talk big.

Just to pass the time, I decided to humour him, or myself, depending on how you see it. I asked, "So, what exactly *is* your business model? How do you make money?"

He hesitated before saying, "Oh, I do a few things here and there, but mainly I help others succeed in their business journeys."

Yeah, right. In my book, a self-proclaimed "mentor" who brags about their own competence is just someone who couldn't make it on their own and now takes credit for others' successes—whether they actually helped or not.

I pointed out that he hadn't given me a single concrete answer during the entire ride. Instead of defending his so-called business, he cleared his throat, stood up, and walked over to the train doors. Another passenger was waiting to get off at the next stop. Without missing a beat, he turned to the new guy and said, "Hey, nice sweater!" Here we go again.

These repeated encounters with scammers are probably why I still have trust issues, even as an adult. No wonder I was struggling to believe anything Alaul was telling me.

I was going over Alaul's messages to me just to make sure I didn't overlook anything. In his last message, he claimed they had sent an official letter to my Australian address requesting my appearance with the bail money, but it was sent through local post and could take over a month to arrive. He practically begged me to come bail Nida out, saying it was unnecessary to keep her locked up for that long, not that I would even consider doing such a thing to my own sister.

Of course it was too expensive. The government had bigger priorities—like using taxpayer money to house hardened criminals in local prisons and provide shelter to refugees selling drugs and committing felonies at the border.

As I boarded my plane, I received another message from Alaul, "*You are coming, right?*"

To which I immediately texted back, "*Yes, Officer Mofiz, I am boarding my flight. See you day after tomorrow.*"

...

I landed in Bangladesh at 11:30 PM four days after Alaul's first message. I had a clear plan: head straight to the police station Alaul mentioned and spend the night with Nida until the court opened in the morning to pay any amount the bail order demanded.

Knowing how most of Bangladesh—especially government offices—still rely on paper transactions requiring cash deposits at specific banks or outlets, I stopped at a money exchange inside the airport to convert dollars equivalent to 4 lakh Bangladeshi taka. Naturally, I got ripped off in the process. The airport exchange always seemed to have an uncanny ability to manipulate forex rates, hiking up the cost of a dollar several times over compared to buying it from an unlicensed street dealer. The real scam wasn't the black-market dealers!

As I accepted the thick bundles of cash, I became painfully aware of how nosy people could be. A few individuals in the queue inched closer, breathing down my neck, their eyes fixated on the money, mentally counting every note before I could stash it away. In my rush to keep prying eyes off the cash, I hastily shoved everything into my luggage—including my passport and travel documents, which I had used during the conversion—without a second thought.

Rolling my small luggage outside to the airport taxi bay, I was immediately swarmed by taxi drivers quoting absurd fares, all claiming their meters were "broken." A classic scam by the fare-based transport syndicate. With ride-sharing services like Uber disrupting their business, they now relied on a door-to-door salesman approach, pitching "competitive" rates to secure passengers straight off international flights.

As I stepped away from the swarm, I noticed an autorickshaw driver sitting calmly in his three-wheeled vehicle, watching on as the taxi drivers circled me like vultures, hoping to score fares in foreign currency. But the frenzy died down the moment I powered on my phone and opened a ride-sharing app. Realising they had lost a potential customer, the taxi drivers quickly moved on to harass the next traveller on the sidewalk.

That's when the autorickshaw driver approached, his movement catching my attention from the corner of my eye.

"Could I offer you a ride, sir?" he asked, his tone surprisingly polite.

"No, thank you. I'm calling for an Uber," I replied curtly, my eyes fixed on my phone.

Unfazed, he persisted, "If you don't mind me asking, how much is the fare showing on your phone?"

I looked up, sceptical. "Why?"

His voice softened, almost pleading, "I could drop you off for fifty takas less than whatever your phone shows. It's been a slow day, and this fare would help me pay the daily rent for leasing the autorickshaw."

I looked at his face—middle-aged, tired eyes, an almost sincere expression. The discount wasn't much, and money wasn't the issue. I figured this could count toward my first good deed of the year in Bangladesh.

"Okay, let's go. You don't need to give me a discount," I told him.

His face lit up. "Right this way," he gestured toward his green autorickshaw.

The vehicle was secured with metal grill doors on both sides, a design meant to prevent passengers from falling out, unlike the older autorickshaws I remembered from my childhood. However, the grills were locked using tower bolts that could only be latched from the driver's side, effectively caging in the passengers. This setup also protected drivers from unruly passengers—a precaution that spoke volumes about the changing times.

The driver got in first, unlocking the latch before the grill door swung open. "Please, sir, get in!"

I climbed into the backseat and held the door closed as he secured it from his side, sliding the bolt in place before we drove off.

On the way, he tried making small talk. Maybe he was bored, or maybe it kept him from falling asleep. Either way, I kept my responses brief, knowing that people here had no concept of social boundaries and would pry into personal matters given the chance.

"Sir, are you a police officer?" he asked, glancing at me through the rearview mirror.

"No. Why?"

He continued, "Then why are you heading straight to the police station from the airport?"

"I'm meeting a relative there," I replied, keeping it vague.

His curiosity was relentless. "Are you a businessman, sir?"

The words "entrepreneur" and "mentor" echoed in my mind as I rolled my eyes at my own thoughts. But I knew what he meant. People often assumed those returning from abroad were either visiting loved ones or managing businesses set up in Bangladesh, where costs were lower and regulations more lenient—at least on paper. The reality was more complicated, with political racketeers extorting "protection" money and local scams inflating costs. Unless, of course, you were politically well-connected.

"No, I'm not," I answered, opening the GPS app on my phone to track our route. I wanted to cut this conversation short.

He pressed on, "So, what do you do, sir?"

I wasn't about to tell him I was a surgeon. Instead, I used the safest, most relatable lie, "I'm a clerk at a company. Nothing fancy."

But he wasn't giving up. "Which country did you come from?"

"Australia," I said, my attention shifting to the scenery outside the metal grills as we entered the narrow streets of Tejgaon's industrial district. Filth lined the road, open sewers ran parallel, and the streets were eerily deserted compared to the bustling market districts that never seemed to close.

That's when I noticed we took a left turn instead of going straight. We were still on course, but the detour seemed longer. "Why aren't we going straight through?" I asked.

The driver smiled, "Road ahead is closed for maintenance."

I brushed it off, knowing how unreliable online map updates were in Bangladesh. Still, a part of me stayed alert as I watched the route closely.

He quieted down just enough for me to believe the small talk sessions were finally over. Just then, the driver spoke up, "Sir, fuel is running low. I'll quickly drive into the fuel station ahead and fill her up."

As annoying as that was, I was in no position to argue. I sighed, "Sure." We pulled up to the station, and he unlatched the doors on both sides of the passenger compartment. "The intake is under the passenger seat, sir. You'll need to step out. But you can leave your belongings in, no problem."

I wasn't about to leave my things unattended. "No, that's okay. Just make it quick, please."

It was almost midnight as I stepped out with my small luggage. I glanced behind and noticed a motorcycle with two scrawny men pulling up. We briefly locked eyes before they circled to the other side of the autorickshaw and stopped beside it. The driver of the motorcycle spoke, "Driver, you shouldn't leave both passenger doors open. It could cause an accident."

The man sitting behind him reached over and pushed the metal frame door closed, his fingers gripping the bars as he peered inside. He held on until the autorickshaw driver returned, latched the door shut, and apologised, "Really sorry about the inconvenience, sirs." The motorcycle then sped off without refuelling at all.

We got back on the road. A little while later, the driver pointed ahead and said, "Sir, there's a woman hailing an autorickshaw. Would you mind if we picked her up? It doesn't feel right to leave her alone at this hour."

I looked over and saw a figure dressed in a full black burkha, only her eyes visible, standing at the side of a dark street, arm raised. A chill ran down my spine as something felt off. The driver was already slowing down, anticipating that my approval would come any second.

"No, keep driving," I said.

He hesitated. "But sir—"

"We didn't agree to share a ride. Keep going."

He pressed the accelerator, and we sped past her. I glanced back but could barely see through the dirty plastic window. Only a faint headlight followed at a distance.

I checked the map on my phone, and my heart sank. We were completely off course. "We're going the wrong way. Turn around now."

He looked at me through the rearview mirror and smiled, "My apologies, sir. I just wanted to take a quick break to relieve myself. This area is quieter to take a piss uninterrupted. I'll only be a moment and then turn around."

My chest began palpating. "No. Do it later at the police station."

"Sir, I can't hold it in. I'm really sorry," he said, ignoring my plea as he pulled over. I tried reasoning with him, even offering an empty water bottle, but he insisted, "I can't do it in a bottle. Just a moment, please."

Before I could object, he flung both passenger doors open, just as he had at the fuel station, and hurried away.

I noticed a shadow stretching in front of the autorickshaw from a single headlight approaching from behind. A motorcycle pulled up. I realised that I put myself into a trap. Running wasn't an option—I wouldn't get far on foot with my belongings. Desperate, I tried to secure the doors, fumbling with the tower bolts on the driver's side.

The autorickshaw's weight shifted. I turned to see one of the men from the fuel station sitting beside me. My pulse quickened. The weight shifted again, and the other man was now on my other side, boxing me in. I realised what was happening—this wasn't just an odd detour. It was a mugging disguised as an autorickshaw ride.

Both men wore cold, emotionless expressions as one of them spoke, his words rehearsed and robotic, as if he'd said them countless times before, "Bag, wallet, and the SIM card from your phone. Now."

I turned toward him and met his hollow eyes. He was just a teenager with his arms covered in rashes—likely a drug addict. They reeked of alcohol and sweat. A sharp poke jabbed my other side, and I turned to find the second man pressing a switchblade against my lower flank, the tip slicing through my shirt, just shy of breaking skin.

The autorickshaw driver climbed back into his seat, locking eyes with me through the rearview mirror. His voice was eerily calm, "I'm sorry for what's about to happen, sir. Hand everything over, and we'll let you go."

Staring at him through the mirror, I tried reasoning, "If it's money you want, I'll give you whatever I have in my wallet. There's nothing in the bag but a change of clothes."

The man with the blade twisted it slightly, just enough to draw a sting as the other addict repeated, "Bag, wallet, and the SIM card."

I let out a defeated sigh and handed over everything they demanded. One of the men pocketed my smaller belongings before climbing out and riding off on the motorcycle. The other remained inside holding my bag with one hand, blade still pressed against me with the other.

The autorickshaw driver spoke again, "Look, sir, I know this isn't what you wanted to experience on your first day back home, but you've been nothing but kind to me. That's why we've decided to let you keep your phone."

I let out a sarcastic sigh. "My faith in humanity has been restored!"

He caught on to my untimely sarcasm. I blame Sufi for ruining my sense of urgency and panic in the face of danger. The driver's annoyance was clear as he continued, "Normally, we just take everything, stab the guy a few times, and leave him by the side of the road."

I couldn't help but ask, "So do you stab them before or *after* they hand everything over?"

The driver looked puzzled for a moment before the man holding the knife to my flank finally answered, "After." He twisted the blade just enough to break my skin, drawing blood.

Ignoring the immediate danger next to me, I let my ridiculous fight-or-flight mechanism take over—bantering with my muggers. I turned back to the driver and asked, "If someone has already handed over everything, what's the point of stabbing them?"

Both men hesitated, briefly questioning their own methods, before the driver snapped, "Get out and walk away. Don't look back."

I sighed. "Fine. You've already taken everything, at least let me grab my passport from my luggage." I needed it—not just for the formalities related to Nida's bail, but for slightly more pressing matters, like, I don't know, getting back to Australia!

The autorickshaw driver exhaled sharply, finally losing patience. "Take his phone and stab him fourteen times."

Fourteen? That seemed oddly specific. That's when it hit me—I had pushed too far.

"Wait, wait, I'm getting off," I said quickly.

I stumbled out of the vehicle, and as soon as my feet touched the ground, the metal door slammed shut. The autorickshaw sped off into the darkness, taking my luggage with it.

Perhaps they had an informant at the airport who marked me as an easy target, feeding them details about my cash exchange. If so, I had taken the bait perfectly.

I spun around to catch the license plate, but there wasn't one—only a painted inscription in Bengali that translated to "Mother's prayers."

Left stranded in an empty industrial district, the reality sank in. I needed to get out before I lost even my phone to a second mugging. I quickly activated my Australian eSIM and turned on international roaming. Only two names came to mind: Shiro and Rajesh. I hadn't been in touch with them since Sufi passed away and hadn't informed them about my visit, so I wasn't sure if they were available. Fortunately, Shiro answered and said he could pick me up, but it would take him an hour to get there.

Standing alone in the dark, I began cancelling all my credit cards through mobile apps, realising with a sinking heart that this would make paying for Nida's bail even more difficult.

It was bad enough that international roaming had abysmal internet speeds—my banking apps were timing out before even opening. I needed to deactivate my cards before my muggers got smart and tapped out heaps of money. As I stood there, frustrated by the sluggish connection, a woman in a black burkha walked up and stopped right next to me, stealing glances from the corner of her eye.

I didn't notice her at first—until I felt the night shift beside me. When I turned my head and saw nothing but a pair of piercing eyes peeking through the veil, I nearly had a mini heart attack.

"Ahh!" I yelped, stepping back.

She remained unfazed. "You look like you're here for a good time. Do you need some company?"

My fright morphed into genuine irritation. I gave her a deadpan stare. "Do I *look* like I'm having the time of my life here? Get out of my face, lady."

In hindsight, I wasn't exactly polite, which wasn't very in line with my adopted country's *live and let live* values. I knew criminals often hid their identities behind the religious dressing. But before I could reflect on my lack of manners, I spotted a large man emerging from the shadows—possibly her pimp. Suddenly, politeness seemed like a survival tactic.

I immediately backtracked. "Uh—sorry, that was rude of me."

I wasn't apologising because I had remembered my upbringing; I was apologizing because self-preservation demanded it. At the same time, I started scanning my surroundings, searching for the glow of a streetlamp or the safety of a building's light—because in my mind, a little illumination might somehow keep the predators at bay.

I moved a few blocks down and sent Shiro my GPS coordinates. His only response was a thumbs-up emoji. I wasn't sure if it was an acknowledgment or passive-aggressive resentment for making him come pick me up from the middle of nowhere without even telling him I was in the country.

I managed to block all my cards and called the Australian consulate to report my stolen passport. Just as I did, my network cut out completely. At least a few things were sorted, I thought.

I sat on the steps of a biscuit factory entrance, huddled under the dim glow of a flickering night light, my chin resting on my hands, contemplating the *stellar* choices that had brought me here. At least the warm, sugary aroma of freshly baked biscuits filled the air—offering the tiniest bit of comfort in an otherwise disastrous night.

Nearly two hours passed before the headlights of a car appeared in the distance, cutting through the darkness as it approached. The vehicle stopped right in front of me and honked its horn.

I couldn't see who was inside, but at this point, you'd think I'd be more cautious. Instead, I resigned myself to fate.

It was either Shiro.

Or a human trafficker.

Yaad | Chapter 2. Playing dress-up

I had enough for one night and decided to hop in. As I opened the passenger-side door, I muttered, "Shiro, you got a new car?" But as the door swung open, my words trailed off.

Seated inside was an athletic male figure with a sharp, clean-shaven jawline, wearing a long-haired wig and a pink floral cocktail dress. I blinked in disbelief, my jaw slightly unhinged.

"Yeah, nah... it's the company car. Quickly, get in," the figure said.

It was Shiro. *Sort of.*

I slid in, shut the door, and could only muster a single word: "What?"

Shiro tried clarifying whatever he thought i was asking, "crime has been through the roof since the ruling party was overthrown by the public last month."

I saw the news—the long-standing dictatorship of the previous ruling party had been overthrown by children and the general public. Now, in a state of relative lawlessness, former political goons who once operated under the payrolls of corrupt politicians had become freelancers of sorts, running scam and crime rings across the country, like the one I became a victim of just hours earlier. Meanwhile, many politically aligned police officers had gone into hiding, fearing that if recognised, they would be beaten to death by the public for siding with the fallen government during the rebellion.

I turned back to the scene before me and asked, "Yeah, times are strange.",

Shiro chuckled. "Well, not as strange as the Kaushal Veni scandal. What's going on there? Did the Turag Curse finally catch up to him and Nida?"

I replied, "I don't know what caught up to whom. All I know is I need to get Nida out of police custody."

Shiro's jaw dropped in disbelief. "Nida? Seriously? I didn't see anything like that on the news. What did she do?"

I shrugged. "Yeah, me neither, and I have no idea. But what's going on *here*?" I gestured toward Shiro, who was wearing makeup and a cocktail dress.

Shiro pulled onto the road, smirking. "Got a job at a multinational company originally based in America that has diversity and LGBTQ+ friendly in their company values. They provide heaps of benefits to their gender and sexually diverse employees—including a bloody company car for safety!"

I furrowed my brows. "Minority?"

Shiro grinned. "Yep."

I took a deep breath and composed myself. "Alright, Shiro. I just... wasn't expecting this. I didn't realise you were transitioning. My apologies."

Shiro burst into laughter. "Transitioning? Mate, no! I was struggling to land a job when I saw an opening at a company that gives special priority to gender minorities."

I laughed. "I'm surprised you haven't been labelled a 'Hijra' and threatened to be stoned to death by our fellow countrymen."

Shiro chuckled. "I don't make a habit of walking around the park in a dress—that would be inviting trouble from the local wannabe gangsters. This façade is strictly for work and professional benefits! That is why I don't even go anywhere straight from work. The only reason I came today was because you got mugged and were in unsafe neighbourhood...I didn't want you to get raped too!"

"Thank you for picking me up."

He nodded his head, "You're most welcome, Yaad."

Shiro drove a bit further before I turned to him, narrowing my eyes in amusement. "So, if this is just a scam, why are you still in costume? It's way too late to be out of work at this hour."

Shiro chuckled, steering into a marketplace where hawkers were setting up their stalls for the next day. Just then, a traffic officer flagged us down. *Of course, they're all hunkered down in the safety of the market's night lights.*

The officer approached, motioning for Shiro to roll down the heavily tinted window. As he did, the sight of his muscular frame wrapped in a floral dress, with oily makeup clinging to his sharp features, made the officer pause.

"What... exactly are you supposed to be?" the officer asked, barely concealing his confusion.

Shiro handed over his license and registration without missing a beat. "What's the charge?" he asked in his natural deep voice, not even trying to sound feminine.

The officer's eyes darted between us before settling on me with a smirk. "This what you're into?" as he pointed to Shiro in all his glory!

I scoffed. "Give me a break. I just got here from overseas and was mugged a few streets down. No one was around, and now here you are, under bright lights and crowded streets, patrolling."

Without even pretending to care, the officer muttered, "That area's not in my patrolling jurisdiction. File a general diary entry at the police station if you have complaints."

Shiro rested his hand on the rolled down door window. "Well... officer... that's where we're heading now, so if you'd let us—"

The officer shushed Shiro by pressing a grimy finger to his lips, smearing his makeup as Shiro pulled back in disgust. "Wait. I need to check the car. Both of you, step out," said the officer.

Shiro hesitated. I knew exactly why—the officer wanted to parade him around in public humiliation. But warrants weren't exactly a thing in Bangladesh traffic stops, and we both valued our time more than our dignity at that moment.

As we stepped out, I whispered, "The car is clean, right?"

Shiro gave me a sharp look. "Obviously."

The officer began his search while we stood at a distance. I leaned in and repeated my earlier question, "Why are you still wearing the dress?"

Shiro glanced at the gawking street vendors on the other side of the road and whispered back, "I was invited to a company afterparty. They want to promote me. Something about 'diverse management.'"

I chuckled. "Come on, Shiro. They're not just promoting you because you decided to identify as a woman."

Shiro's smirk widened. "That is *exactly* why I got promoted. There was a guy who did way more work than me, but they laid him off because he didn't fit the company's new diversity policy. And I don't identify as a woman."

I blinked. "What?"

Shiro grinned. "This was supposed to be a joke. In the job application, I put my name as *Marcellina Williams* and my gender as 'other.' In the blank space, I wrote, 'I identify as a tree.' When they called me for an interview, I thought I'd take it further and showed up in a dress. Next thing I know, I'm hired as *Treefolk Marcellina*. Hundreds of applications with my real resume got ignored, but this?" He gestured to himself. "Got me a job instantly. God bless Western values!"

Before I could respond, the officer rummaging through the trunk looked up. "If you just arrived from overseas, where's your luggage?"

I wasn't sure if he was being sarcastic. "I was mugged a few roads down."

The officer mumbled something to himself before resuming his search.

I turned back to Shiro. "I have no idea how you're pulling off this double life. Hasn't anyone caught on?"

Shiro shrugged. "All the locals see through my charade, but they can't say anything because the company policies are dictated in America. They did a background check and all I had to say was 'I am transitioning' and boom! I started getting paid at my usual bank account. One guy in Accounting mocked me and threatened to undress me in public, metaphorically obviously, and expose me as a scam. The company fired him immediately and gave me this tinted car for protection."

I smirked. "And now you're up for a promotion."

Shiro grinned. "Don't hate the player, hate the game."

I sighed. "Alright, but I lost everything in the mugging. I need your help withdrawing money. I'll transfer it to your account, and you can take it out for me."

"Of course. You're an idiot for taking an autorickshaw at *this* hour amidst the worst political unrest of the decade. Why didn't you let us know?"

I admitted, "It's complicated. Even I don't understand the full extent of this mess. All I know is that Nida is being held for allegedly stabbing Kaushal."

Shiro's expression darkened, which looked silly under the smeared makeup. "Is your brother-in-law..."

I replied, "It was a box cutter, so he is apparently fine."

The officer, now done with the search, straightened up. "Everything's clear. Go to the police station and report your stolen passport. You don't want a criminal pasting their photo over yours and using it to leave the country."

I started to say, "That's not how it works anymore—"

Shiro nudged me, shaking his head. "We'll continue this conversation in the car."

Without arguing, I let it go. Shiro retrieved his documents, and as we drove off, the street vendors erupted into giggles behind us.

Almost within minutes, we were stuck behind a queue of long-haul trucks entering the city to drop off daily trade. The notorious late-night industrial district traffic had us locked in place. In Dhaka, the only good times to travel seemed to be right before midnight or at dawn—any other time, and even a few kilometres could take hours.

Shiro sighed. "Well, this is going to take a while. There's an ATM up ahead somewhere. You can transfer the money to me, and I'll withdraw it for you."

I hesitated. "Will the transfer be instantaneous?"

Shiro paused, then laughed. "What was I thinking? Of course not. It'll take weeks. But "How much do you need? I'll lend it to you."

When I told him the exact amount, he twitched, "Yaad, the company's diversity mascot doesn't make that kind of money," he said, gesturing to himself. "The only person who probably could've covered that sum was Rajesh, but he's... away, in a manner of speaking."

I shrugged. "What other way is there for me to withdraw money? I can't go through the official route—I don't have any ID on me."

Shiro fell silent for a moment, as if considering something. Then he pulled out his phone and started scrolling through his contacts, barely touching the accelerator as the car inched forward every minute. There was no point in telling him it wasn't safe to use his phone while driving—where we were, a driver was more likely to die of boredom than from distraction.

After a moment, he spoke up. "If you can get someone to pay a guy in Australia, I can have a *Hundi* here pay you the equivalent in Bangladeshi Taka."

I understood the slang. A "*Hundi*" was essentially a street money broker, part of an informal and highly efficient network moving cash across borders. Technically illegal, but relied upon by thousands—migrant workers, international students, and businessmen alike—who needed to send money quickly without waiting for the Bangladeshi treasury to release funds after taking a hefty cut. Western Union and similar services were too expensive, leaving a massive market gap that *Hundi*s gladly filled.

Of course, there were risks. *Hundis* operated in a legal grey area, skirting financial regulations by greasing the right palms—usually local council members or police officers who conveniently looked the other way. But if a *Hundi* had a slow month and failed to pay their dues, law enforcement would crack down hard. The broker would disappear overnight, taking the money of those unfortunate enough to have trusted them. And since using their services was illegal to begin with, victims had nowhere to turn.

To avoid being caught, *Hundis* operated strictly on a referral basis. No one walked in off the street and asked for a deal—you had to be vouched for. It was almost like being initiated into some elite underground network.

I turned to Shiro, raising an eyebrow. "So... how exactly do you know a *Hundi*?"

Shiro smiled nervously. "Yeah, well... when I was struggling to land a job here, some locals told me how I could 'study' at a Western college for a fraction of the cost, work there, and, you know... stay indefinitely."

I gave him a look. I knew exactly what he was talking about.

Ghost colleges and *Visa factories*.

For those unfamiliar, these were so-called educational institutions that existed primarily to issue student visas. They lured in international students with promises of minimal academic pressure, cheap tuition, and extended work opportunities. Too good to be true? It usually was.

Many students who come through these channels focus less on studying and more on working trade jobs—roles locals are often better suited for, or the booming food delivery gigs. These students are frequently content with underpaid work, often working illegally in cash jobs with unscrupulous employers eager to sidestep weekend surcharges. As a result, their academics suffer, and "upstanding members" of the immigrant community are often called in to remind these "fake students" that neglecting their studies could lead to visa cancellations.

Truth be told, most of these students are laser-focused on the ultimate goal: permanent residency. It didn't matter how many academic warnings they received; the promise of an indefinite stay in a prosperous Western country while being able to support their family overseas with their meagre earnings outweighed everything else, even if it meant driving a taxi for the rest of their lives.

I couldn't hold back my laughter. "What happened next, Marcellina?"

Shiro sighed. "I applied with my actual name—Shiro Edwards, man. This was before I knew Treefolk Marcellina would take off. Otherwise, I would've applied for a scholarship under that name!"

I nodded in disbelief. "Okay... and then what happened?"

He continued, "I paid a 'study agent' some money, and they took care of the rest. The guy filled out my visa application with all sorts of bogus information. He said it was fine because everyone who went through them did it."

That was fraud, but there was no point in telling Shiro that. Do I blame these students for trying to improve their lives through whatever means they could? No. But their choices create challenges for others. Actions like these fuel distrust, making it harder for genuine students to secure opportunities. Worse, degrees from these so-called "ghost colleges" hold little value when it comes to skilled employment. The real culprits are the agents and businesspeople who run these visa factories and hack agencies.

I pressed on. "So, Shiro, what happened next?"

"I got my visa, left, and started school at a college that was on top of a strip club, shared its space with a gym, and had five chairs and a whiteboard!"

I chuckled, "That must have been *scenic*! Were the faculty members...erm, *exotic*?"

Shiro continued, "The only tutor there wouldn't stop talking about how 'progressive' she was, proudly sharing how she 'enabled' her ten-year-old son's transition to a girl by having the doctors inject female hormones into him just because he liked playing with dolls and wearing dresses. I thought that was child abuse—the kid should be allowed to decide for themselves when they're an adult. Can you imagine someone like that tutoring our course?"

I followed up. "What subject did you enrol in?"

He dodged the question. "Subject? No idea, man. I asked the other students what their plans were—most of them barely spoke English. One said 'food delivery', another said 'farmhand', and the majority said 'Taxi.' I didn't want to do any of that!"

I rolled my eyes. "So what exactly did you do, Shiro?"

Shiro laughed. "Well, I found work at a Yiros shop making rotisserie chicken wraps!"

I asked, "And was that easier or harder than the alternatives?"

He grinned. "Easier. I just made up fake experience from a number of South Asian countries on my résumé. Who was going to check? Besides, I was paid in cash, so the employer was happy paying me less, and I didn't have to worry about student visa work restrictions."

I knew Shiro's type and wasn't fond of them. These were the people who fabricated overseas experience to land casual jobs, despite never having lifted a finger in their lives. Predictably, they'd underperform and get reprimanded regularly.

I sighed. "Please tell me you at least studied and finished your degree."

Shiro chuckled. "Yeah, well... about that. So, I got into an argument with the European Yiros shop owner—he tried to shortchange me on a Sunday surcharge. Let's just say things got a little physical. The bast*rd cheated his way into the immigration system years ago, so he had the upper hand. He made me pay for a whole heap of things that... well, ultimately led to my student visa being cancelled and me being deported."

I wasn't particularly enjoying this conversation, but I tried connecting the dots. "So your 'agent' referred you to the *Hundi* so your family could send you money?"

Shiro smirked. "Yeah, that's right. Though, looking back, that was a bad investment. Oh well, you win some, you lose some."

I wouldn't call that an investment—more like a scam.

In my view, immigrants fall into two broad categories. There are the genuine ones—the ones who give their all, pushing against the odds to build a better future. And then there are the others—the ones who fabricate entire lives, take on jobs they're completely unqualified for, and lack even the most basic social awareness. These people tarnish the reputation of immigrants as a whole. Worse, their failures overshadow the achievements of the hardworking ones, leaving many of us fighting against stereotypes.

Still, as social beings, we're expected to integrate, to interact. Failing to do so risks being labeled antisocial. Unfortunately, these individuals could be seen as the immigrant counterparts to what some might stereotype as 'bogans' in Australia or 'rednecks' in America.

We accepted these trade-offs. We left behind a life in Bangladesh filled with endless queues for government services, middlemen demanding bribes for anything official, and constant political manoeuvring just to get basic things done. In exchange, we found ourselves in a lonely, individualistic society where the biggest concerns often revolve around alcohol addiction, gambling, and people exploiting the mental health system and unemployment benefits for an easy payout.

...

After a few minutes of silently tapping on his phone, Shiro spoke up. "I sent my *Hundi* contact a message, and he sent me the bank details of someone in Australia. Get someone to transfer the money to the *Hundi*'s contact there, and I'll collect the Taka equivalent from the

Hundi here and bring it to you at the police station first thing in the morning."

I thanked him as I pulled out my phone and started messaging Lily about the whole ordeal.

After a while, Shiro said, "So, uh... tell me about you. Rajesh and I were almost certain we'd never see you again."

"Sorry I lost touch," I replied.

He chuckled. "No need to apologise. Honestly, I saw it coming after Sufi passed away. Truth be told, I'm glad we ran into each other again, even if it's under... unusual circumstances with the whole Kaushal Veni scandal." He adjusted the dress he was wearing, as if readjusting a bra underneath. I decided not to ask too many questions.

I changed the subject. "So, where's Rajesh?"

"Long story short - In hiding. he decided working a job was too hard and said he'd rather go into politics for an easy way out."

I raised an eyebrow. "I didn't know Rajesh was into politics."

Shiro chuckled. "I don't think he is. But he has the family money to like or dislike whatever he pleases. And he figured out that all he had to do was chant some political slogans, take pictures with the right people, and—boom!—he's important enough to be entrusted with funds that he can embezzle to buy houses in Singapore and the Middle East."

I smirked. "Didn't realise it was that easy to break into politics without actually holding any position."

Shiro smirked back. "It isn't. But if you've got money, you can buy your way in. You can even buy votes by handing out some money to victims affected by natural disasters. And the best way in? Through people you know."

"Like?" I prompted.

Shiro grinned. "Apparently, Sufi had an uncle—Khokon. Some bigshot political leader in a small town up north in Gaibandha. Rajesh got in touch with him through Sufi's mom, and Khokon invited him to a few inner political meetings."

I frowned. "A politician helping someone out of the goodness of his heart? What's the catch?"

Shiro laughed. "There's always a catch, isn't there? Rajesh told me his timing was perfect. Khokon had screwed up some dam project, and it ended up flooding entire croplands. Government repair payouts were taking forever, so he needed a 'loan' to stop the flooding before the start of his election campaign. Rajesh lent him the money, and Khokon returned the favour by getting him a ticket into politics..."

"...And worked his way up from there," I finished for him. "Funny how even the easy way still involves work. Rajesh picked a really bad time to go into politics."

Shiro chuckled. "He went in bragging about how Khokon hadn't lost a council election in two decades and that he was a shoo-in for the big leagues through him. He joined Khokon's office—part of the ruling political party—just two months before the protests that toppled the dictatorship. A fair council election was held in Gaibandha a week later, and Khokon lost by a landslide. The new council member immediately went after him for fraud in the dam construction project, so Khokon went into hiding... and Rajesh had to follow because he'd just sworn his allegiance."

I smirked. "So, in short, Rajesh's political career ended before it even started."

We both laughed before Shiro turned to me and said, "Alright, doctor. Fill me in. What have you been up to?"

So I told him about my life in Australia and how I met Lily. But I left out certain details—how I had been back during Sufi's final days and how I'd held onto Sufi's diary for a while. Some things were better left unsaid.

Yaad | Chapter 3. Double standards

We finally pulled up in front of the police station. As I opened my door, I noticed Shiro still sitting in the driver's seat, unmoving.

"You're not coming with me?" I asked.

"Not while wearing a dress and makeup," he replied, gesturing at himself. "Especially not into a police station."

I smirked. "Come on now, you look beautiful, Treefolk Marcellina!"

Shiro scoffed. "Apparently, beauty standards are set by women for themselves and other women. My 'hyperfeminist' work colleague says that when a man compliments a random woman for her looks, it's objectification!"

I tilted my head in amusement. "Oh, my apologies, Shiro. I didn't realise I was objectifying you."

He laughed. "Well, a small cohort of women objectify themselves by dressing in a way that attracts attention and then complain when men they don't find attractive try to flirt with them. Funny enough, they rarely seem to have an issue when it's someone they consider good-looking. I should know—women who rolled their eyes at Rajesh's advances usually don't seem to mind me... erm... when I'm dressed more appropriately, obviously."

He paused for a moment, his smile disappearing for a moment as he continued, "Then there are others—the ones who try to match the beauty of the woman their partner is gawking at, driven by insecurity. Honestly, they deserve better partners."

I tried to lighten the sudden change in Shiro's mood. "And which category do you fall under?"

Shiro sighed. "Neither. I'm just a tired man looking for an easy way out, and I'm not ashamed to admit it." He stretched, then added, "I'll see you in the morning with the money—dressed properly."

I was genuinely grateful. "Thanks, Shiro. See you in the morning."

As I walked toward the police station doors, my phone buzzed with a message from Lily: *Money is sent, here's the receipt.*

I turned around, thinking to let Shiro know—but he had already driven away so I forwarded the receipt to Shiro's number. He sent me another thumbs-up emoji!

As I approached the police station door, I noticed a middle-aged woman sitting on the porch in a crisp salwar kameez. Her thick jet-black hair was neatly groomed, but her eyes looked weary. As I walked past, she muttered, "Everyone here is corrupt! I've been trying to talk to my innocent husband since this afternoon, but they won't even let me see him. All they want is the kind of money that our modest family can't afford!"

I took note of her words but chose not to let them shape my expectations. Other people's experiences shouldn't dictate our biases—only prepare us for what might happen. I simply replied, "Thank you for letting me know. I'll be cautious."

Inside, only one officer was at the desk, dozing off and jerking awake at awkward angles. I walked up and sat in the chair in front of him, which startled him awake.

"I'm here for Nida Oman," I said.

The officer pointed lazily toward the cells. "You must be the brother. Last one on the right. But Mofiz Sir is handling her case. He said that he will drop by in the morning so you'll have to wait until then."

I thanked him. "Can I talk to her?"

He barely nodded, waving a hand as if to say, *Do whatever you want.*

At that point, I decided to bring up the mugging. "Oh, and I was mugged in an autorickshaw. They took my wallet, SIM card, suitcase, and passport."

The desk officer looked at me blankly, as if trying to figure out why I was telling him this, before groggily realizing that he was, in fact, a police officer. "Oh, you're filing a report! Please tell me it wasn't in this neighbourhood," he said, secretly hoping it wouldn't fall under his jurisdiction and add more paperwork to his uneventful night shift.

"Yes, it was," I replied.

He let out a long sigh and muttered something under his breath as he rummaged through his drawers. Finally, he pulled out a form and placed it on the desk, grumbling, "I had to jinx it. Just when I thought I'd finally caught up with the backlog and could get some rest..."

Then, looking at me, he said, "Quickly fill this out, and we should be okay. The instructions are on the last page."

I sat down and filled out the relatively straightforward form while he drifted in and out of sleep. The moment I finished, he stirred, as if sensing I was done.

"All good?" he asked.

"Yes," I replied.

"Good," he said, taking the form from me and gesturing toward the jail corridor. "Now go see your sister."

As I made my way across the corridor of cells, a man suddenly jumped up, rushing to the bars screaming. "Hey, you there! How did they let you in while my wife has been crying outside all day, begging to see me?"

I had no answer for him. "I'm sorry, sir, I don't know. Best to ask the officers."

His agitation grew. "All rude and corrupt bast*rds! Tell me, what did you say to the officer to get in?"

"I simply asked to see my sister, and he agreed."

The man scoffed. "Well, see, my wife asked the same! I don't understand this double standard! I'm Hafiz Ali, a respected businessman who only wants the best for this country, yet they do horrible things to innocent men like me just because I was loyal to the previous political party!"

His rant spiralled into a political monologue, chanting slogans to flaunt his allegiance to people who clearly didn't care. "You can break my body, but not my heart! My heart belongs to the party that ruled this country for decades, and it will make a comeback when everything inevitably falls apart!"

It was high time to walk away from this fascist lunatic. As I stepped past him, his authoritative tone cracked into desperation. "Please... I need to speak to my wife. It's urgent. Ask the officer at the desk—please... please."

His wailing was more irritating than anything, when suddenly a voice rang out from the last cell.

"Just go talk to the officer, please," Nida said. "This man has been murmuring that he's innocent for the last *two* days. I don't care if he is or not—I just need some peace. I can't focus with his silent wailing."

I sighed. "Sure."

Turning back to Hafiz, I said, "I'll see what I can do."

His face lit up. "Thank you, good man! May your good deed be returned in plenty."

I didn't bother responding and walked back to the officer at the desk.

"So, that man—Hafiz, in the cell..." I began.

The officer mumbled, half-asleep and probably saying more than he was authorised to. "Claims he's innocent and all that. Conveniently forgot to mention that his wife tried bribing me seven times since we locked him up this afternoon to sneak a phone into his cell. Said he needed to make a call. But we've got strict orders—no contact with the outside or electronic devices until further instructions. He's charged with wire fraud, and intelligence says he could tamper with internet evidence or something."

I smirked. "So you didn't take the bribe?"

"Of course not. Not everyone in the force is as corrupt as the media makes us out to be. If you don't believe me, go ask his wife."

So I did.

Outside, Hafiz's wife admitted she had, in fact, tried to bribe the officer. "It was necessary," she said, completely contradicting her earlier claims.

It's funny how people spin a story to serve their own purpose.

When I confronted Hafiz, he refused to say another word, slumping back into his cell. The officer at the desk laughed. "See? Told you!"

I walked back to Nida's cell, and as I approached, she let out a dramatic sigh. "Finally, some peace!"

Standing in front of her now, I took in the sight of a middle-aged woman with curly auburn hair tied back into a ponytail, stray wavy locks framing her face as if they hadn't been brushed in ages. Her sunken eyes, shadowed by dark circles, and her hollowed cheeks made her look like she had aged far beyond her years. She had lost a noticeable amount of weight since I last saw her just a few years ago. She wore an odd turtleneck half-sleeved sweater dress and thermal tights—an outfit that wouldn't have stood out if it weren't the middle of summer. As she leaned forward, her skinny arms stretched through the bars to hug me.

"You took your sweet time! I was almost..." she said, her voice trailing off as she gradually loosened her grip on the hug. It felt like she was distracted, as if she were speaking to someone else I couldn't see. Was she talking to herself?

I sighed. "I was mugged, lost my passport, all my cards and your bail money."

She asked, "Are you okay?"

"Just a nick. Nothing major." I waved it off. "The desk officer said that Alaul Mofiz will be back in the morning, and Shiro will be here tomorrow with the money."

"Then go find a hotel and get some rest, Yaad. I'll be here."

I sighed again. "As it happens, I don't even have an ID to check into a hotel. So I guess you're stuck with me for the night."

Nida chuckled. "Then I suppose I'm lucky. You're the only person who came for me."

I held up a finger, motioning for her to wait, then turned to the officer at the desk. "It's okay if I stay here with my sister for the night, right?"

The officer barely looked up. "Yeah, sure. Knock yourself out."

Hafiz screeched from his cell. "What? The double standards in this country!"

Almost to rub it in, the officer called back to me, "You can sit inside the cell with the inmate if you want, or just grab a chair and make yourself comfortable outside."

I appreciated the gesture and chose the latter, pulling up a chair next to Nida's cell.

If I ignored the bars between us, it almost felt like old times.

As we sat there face to face, I asked her, "Is it true?"

She leaned in slightly and asked politely, "Could you come a little closer, Yaad? I can't hear you."

Right, I had almost forgotten—she was nearly deaf in one ear. Instead of raising my voice and disturbing the quiet, her suggestion made far more sense.

I pulled my chair closer to the bars, my knees now touching the cold metal. Nida knelt on the floor, sitting as close to me as possible. Realizing it might be more comfortable, I pushed my chair aside and mimicked her posture, sitting cross-legged on the other side of the bars. Our legs pressed against the cold metal as we faced each other.

"Is it true? That you attacked Kaushal?" I repeated.

Nida smiled faintly. "That's much better. I can hear you clearly now."

She took a deep breath as if preparing to defend herself—then exhaled sharply, her shoulders slumping in defeat. She nodded. "Yes. But he attacked first. I was defending myself."

Her tone and the buildup didn't sound convincing to me. I hesitated before pressing further. "I'm sorry...He never seemed like the type."

Nida asked flatly. "And what exactly are you basing that on?"

I shrugged. "On the massive wedding photo in your living room—where you and Kaushal were absurdly posing, staring off into the distance."

She chuckled. "That's how wedding photos are taken, silly. It's artistic. A shame, though—some wedding photographs printed on the cheapest quality paper last longer than the marriage itself."

I asked, "Samira is still with Kaushal's mother?"

"Yes. Samira and our cat, Corporal."

I chuckled. "Corporal? First Sergeant the dog, now Corporal the cat?"

Nida laughed. "Yeah."

I returned to the real question. "So what exactly happened?"

Nida sighed. "It all started with Beebo. I thought with the right care, he could do better. I really thought I could help him."

I knew Nida had told me that Beebo got involved in some really bad things, but she had intentionally left out a lot of the details including the full reason why he was asked to leave home, no matter how many times I asked. I had chalked it up to her not wanting to burden me, especially with me being so far away. But now, I couldn't shake the nagging curiosity about what Sufi had written in his diary—about Beebo and about what had happened to Nida.

I was hoping tonight would finally bring me some answers.

A tear rolled down her cheek as her voice cracked. I gestured her with my hands to take it easy as she composed herself and continued.

Nida | Chapter 4. Influencer

An obnoxiously loud sound was blaring from Beebo's room. Pregnancy had made me even less tolerant of loud noises, so I got out of bed and slowly walked toward his half-open door. Beebo had grown into a tall, lean teenager with a round face, a patchy mustache—denser on one side than the other—and freckles scattered across his skin. He had a high hairline that made it look like he was balding, complemented by sparse, short hair. Pushing the door open slightly, I saw teenage Beebo lying on his side, a smartphone in his hand, watching yet another online video. The voice in the video proclaimed, *"This is my daily routine to becoming a millionaire!"*

I rolled my eyes. Lately, all Beebo had been watching were these so-called "self-help" guides on getting rich—videos made by people who claimed they had cracked the code to success and were now the proud owners of mansions and Ferraris. He used to show them to me, completely enamoured by the flashy cars and sprawling houses, trying to mimic their routines in hopes of achieving the same.

At one point, he started asking me to buy specific diaries and planners—ones recommended by these so-called "rich" influencers. It didn't take long for me to realise that selling these overpriced day planners was a business in itself. They preyed on people who did nothing productive, convincing them that a fancy notebook would somehow get them out of bed and magically tackle their to-do lists for them.

I did not object at first, thinking that if buying a planner motivated Beebo to make real plans and be more productive outside of school, it might be worth it. But time and time again, he would fill out only the first two pages before abandoning it, leaving yet another expensive book to serve as a makeshift support block for a wobbly piece of furniture. After one too many pointless purchases, we started saying no.

Beebo was heartbroken but didn't seemed to recognise the futility of it all. He didn't see that productivity didn't come from the overpriced planners that he bought off affiliate links provided by influencers—it came from discipline, something no amount of aesthetic stationery could buy.

The poor kid also didn't realise that most of these people flaunting their wealth online were either drowning in debt or coasting off family money. Their "advice" was nothing more than vague motivational fluff—wake up early, take a hot shower, hit the gym, send a few emails, go out for expensive dinners—then they'd cut the video short, leaving viewers hanging and pushing them to buy their *exclusive* success book.

I knew these videos were short, just long enough to get monetised, so I waited for it to end. Beebo always got completely absorbed in them, ignoring everything and everyone until the screen went dark. A few minutes later, the video wrapped up with the so-called millionaire saying, *"For more life-changing advice from Tom the Teenage Millionaire, be sure to subscribe and hit the bell icon! Don't miss my next video, where I'll teach you how dining at fancy restaurants will instantly boost your social standing and impress those classy ladies!"*

I cringed. Of course, minors were impressionable and ate this stuff up. The worst part? You couldn't even block these so-called 'financial education' videos with parental controls—if you blocked one, another scammer would pop up elsewhere. For every legitimate financial educator teaching kids about stocks and bonds, there were fifty self-proclaimed influencers flaunting fake wealth, teaching nothing but how to *burn* money instead of building it.

Beebo finally noticed me standing inches away from his bed and looked up as I spoke.

"Beebo, please keep the noise down. Even if you don't want to think about me and baby Samira in my belly, at least think about Kaushal's elderly mother in the other room."

Beebo gave me a cartoonishly confused look, an expression he had probably picked up from one of his videos. "But it wasn't that loud!"

He had developed a habit of arguing his point even when he was wrong, thanks to Tom the Teenage Millionaire, who once said, *'Stand your ground and believe in yourself to become a millionaire.'* Beebo must have taken that advice too literally, failing to realise that successful people also listen to advice and adjust accordingly. For him, Tom was an idol—whatever that fraud said was gospel to Beebo.

I sighed. "Beebo, you couldn't hear how loud it was, but I'm partially deaf, and even I heard it from the other room."

Beebo laughed at my mention of being partially deaf as he always thought I was making a medical condition up just like the other guardians who made excuses to get their wards to behave. I tried to be firm. "We bought you headphones for a reason. Use them. I don't want to hear any sound coming from your room."

He made an annoyed face but reluctantly put on his headphones, then switched to Tom's fan page and logged in. I noticed his account logged in with a flashing pop-up notification that read *'Top Contributor.'* There was no point in dragging this out. My back was already aching from the weight of little Samira in my belly. The doctors had warned that my last trimester could be complicated because of how she was positioned, and I had been advised to take extra time off work and stay on bed rest before they eventually cut me open and pulled her out.

I walked back to my room, lay down, and gradually dozed off.

...

I woke up to Kaushal gently shaking me. He looked stressed and distracted.

"Nida, I have been asked to do something at work today that I'm not comfortable with."

Still groggy, I asked, "What happened?"

"The board called me in about the Turag Project."

I tried to recall what he had said about the Turag Project. My pregnancy brain had been making everything a blur lately, but eventually, it came back to me.

The Turag Project was a mega motorway initiative the government had been trying to complete for decades to ease traffic congestion in the capital. However, corruption and constant tender handovers between contractors loyal to different political parties and government officials had stalled its progress. Numerous government-appointed overseers had taken on the responsibility of completing the project, each instantly becoming a media figure as the supposed savior of Dhaka's notorious traffic problem—only to inevitably fail within their five-year tenures. Some didn't even last that long, fading from the spotlight within a year or two as the media sensationalised the project's history, dubbing it "cursed" with dramatic claims that "all who lead the Turag Project eventually disappear or perish!"—a clear exaggeration.

Now, with growing public pressure and social media making it harder for the government to control the narrative amid rising frustrations over the fascism-dominated public workforce, officials decided to hand the project over to Sigmoid, a private megastructure construction company. This move allowed the government to distance itself from direct responsibility, using Sigmoid as a scapegoat that could be severed without consequence when the project inevitably fails again. Kaushal thought that shifting responsibility also meant that the government could just shrug their shoulders and deflect blame when political influencers started pointing fingers during the next election cycle.

I had always laughed at his concerns, telling him he was overthinking. The elections had not been fair to begin with—votes had been fabricated for more than a decade—so scapegoating seemed unnecessary.

Kaushal, as a senior project manager at Sigmoid with expertise in both civil engineering and computer science, knew a great deal about the project and it's history. The Turag Project was the focus of his undergraduate thesis in Civil Engineering—a topic that nearly cost him his degree due to the severe lack of publicly available information. Naturally when he got to know that Sigmoid will be taking over the construction, he had mixed feelings. He told me at the time the news was circulated throughout the company that the deal seemed rushed. None of the critical details had been shared with the teams in project acquisition—just vague assurances that "the bosses were handling it personally" because it was the *deal of a lifetime.*

I pulled myself out of my thoughts and back to Kaushal's original statement about the board calling him in.

I frowned. "What did the board want with your team?"

"Not the entire team—just me."

That caught me off guard. I slowly sat up. "Why just you?"

Kaushal sighed. "Remember how I told you that seven different teams, including mine, were supposed to handle all the accounts and databases for the Turag Project during the handover from the government to Sigmoid, but we barely received anything of substance?"

"Yes, I remember. What about it?"

"We weren't still being given access to all the records. So, I put in a formal request for access to the project details and agreements. The regional manager told me they weren't widely accessible yet. That made no sense, considering my team was responsible for assessing compliance risks and asset transfers. So, I explained why I needed them this early on."

I had to make sure. "Did you phrase it nicely, Kaushal? You have a habit of being too blunt sometimes."

Kaushal forced a small smile. "Yes, I used corporate jargon. Plenty of *pleases* and *thank you for your consideration.*"

I chuckled. "And?"

"My boss agreed that the seven teams should have access to *all* the documents, so he brought it up with upper management and the board."

Being the person that I was, I immediately jumped to the most logical conclusion before letting him finish. "And they said no?"

Kaushal shot me a playful deadpan look. "For once, Nida, let me finish."

I smirked. "Okay, okay, continue."

"They only gave *me* access to the records and databases," he said, "but I was told I wasn't allowed to discuss them with anyone outside a few specific individuals, my own boss not included. *And* If I found anything, I had to go *directly* to the board."

That caught me off guard. "Isn't that a good thing for your career? You're bypassing all the usual red tape and getting direct access to important people."

Kaushal shook his head. "No, Nida. You don't just *jump* chains of command for something as massive as the Turag Project—especially when it has such a bad reputation. Not to mention there were other managers in who are academically more qualified."

I tilted my head. "But Turag was your thesis project, you're great at analysing and adapting to changing trends, and you told me that most employees at Sigmoid just follow a set rulebook all the way to retirement. You actually know things about the Turag Project while others would probably wing things with their so-called experience. Not to mention that your colleagues probably earned their degrees by memorising PowerPoint slides, while you were in the workforce gaining real experience. I can't think of anyone else who should be allowed early access to the Project's internals."

Kaushal remained quiet as he listened to me trying to make sense of this.

I continued, "Maybe the regional manager put in a good word for you, and this is a sign they trust you with something this big."

Kaushal mumbled, "He didn't seem too happy about the board's decision... and being instructed to withhold information from everyone—preventing team members from communicating during the critical early stages of a rushed deal—didn't sit right with me."

Then, Kaushal looked down at my belly, probably thinking about Samira. "Well, the records will be on my desk tomorrow, and I've already been given access to the digital database. Let's see what I find."

"Good, as long as you get paid for it!" I continued, "Now don't forget, you need to take me to the doctor tomorrow afternoon for my final monthly follow-up. I don't want to be late like last time!"

Kaushal chuckled. "Yes, only one more month until baby Samira comes out! I'll be sure to put my keys and wallet on the bedside table this time. I swear they just grow legs and walk away!"

...

The days began flying by as Kaushal dug deeper into the files he had been given access to, bringing work home almost every night. He became so engrossed that he stopped noticing what was happening around the house, leaving me with two "children" who refused to listen—Beebo and now him. I worked from home most of the time which gave me the flexibility of working out of my bed. Fortunately, Kaushal's mother was there to keep me company, even if her age prevented her from helping with anything too strenuous. At least I had someone to talk to while I handled the daily chores, like doing the laundry and washing the dishes left behind by Beebo and Kaushal.

We had a maid who came in the mornings to cook and mop the floors—tasks I considered the most physically demanding with my altered taste and enlarged belly. We let her in early in the morning, and as she began cooking, she would prepare breakfast for Kaushal and Beebo before they left for the day. After that, she would clean the house and leave before noon. But beyond that, I was left to manage everything else around the house on my own. Meanwhile, Kaushal kept muttering that none of the numbers in the documents were adding up, though he didn't have enough information yet to make complete sense of it. When I pressed him for details, he would either ignore me completely, too absorbed in the paperwork, or give me half-answers, promising to tell me more soon.

Days turned into weeks. Then, one evening, Kaushal finally came to me and laid everything out. The financial records were riddled with discrepancies—annual audits had consistently overlooked critical details, and payments had been made to employees who had long since passed away, their pensions rerouted to offshore accounts. There were even individuals who had been on the payroll for nearly two decades, yet there were no records of them ever having held an actual position.

It was all leading to one conclusion: a large-scale corporate fraud, likely baked into the project itself, and naturally not included in public records. Kaushal and I agreed that the board had probably assured the ruling party they would take on the project, along with all its baggage, as part of securing the deal. And now, Kaushal wasn't being asked to expose the corruption—he was being asked to quietly identify loose ends which the board can clean up before the project was rolled out company-wide.

Kaushal spent several sleepless nights compiling a report, listing every loophole, every financial irregularity, and every political and corporate figure whose name was tied to the off-the-books transactions. I was due for surgery in a week, and the thought of him handing over such a damning document terrified me. I begged him to leave out the names and instead present his findings in the most neutral way possible.

I stayed up with him at night, helping him refine his presentation. I advised him to slip in a few solutions—proposals on how he himself could sort out the mess. My priority was making sure the father of my soon-to-be-born child wasn't deemed expendable. If he played his cards right, this could even secure him an important position within the project.

Naturally, Kaushal was opposed to the idea, calling it immoral and unethical. But politics and corruption are never black and white—only murky shades of grey. The way I saw it, there were only two options as Kaushal wasn't going to let this go:

Option one: Kaushal exposed the corruption and debunked the "curse", the media had a field day, and the public went into an outrage. Important figures fled the country, the project was suspended indefinitely, and we spent the rest of our lives looking over our shoulders, waiting for someone to come after our family for snitching. And even then, the public would forget all about it the moment a pop star eating her own booger made headlines.

Then option two: Kaushal leveraged the information to secure a good position within the project, ensured its completion that would inevitably help millions of people, and avoided feeding a public that didn't care about the lives at stake—only the scandal itself.

And sure enough, when Kaushal presented his findings, he did exactly as I had advised. He walked out of that meeting as the *Chief Overseer* of the Turag Project, with all the financial benefits that came with the promotion.

Within a day, the company's media representatives started arriving at our home, prepping Kaushal for a series of press briefings. He was gradually being positioned as the face of the project—and, in hindsight, the face of all accountability for something with a terrible reputation.

Kaushal's school friends joked that he was "taking the curse onto himself," placing bets on how long he'd last in the role. Most assumed he'd step down within a year, completely unaware of why the project was considered "cursed" in the first place. I always pushed back against their teasing—if anyone could complete that project, it was Kaushal.

Beebo and I would stand quietly in the corner as Kaushal was interviewed in our living room by every major news outlet in the country. They all asked the same question: how did he plan to bring the Turag Project to fruition when no one had managed to complete it in decades? As morally upright as Kaushal was, he understood his priorities—keeping his family safe. And with his expertise, charisma, and ability to say exactly what was necessary—from memorising scripts that I had carefully prepared for him, he quickly became a prominent media figure.

After baby Samira was born, the maternity ward overflowed with massive bouquets of flowers and fruit baskets, all sent by influential politicians and Sigmoid board members, congratulating us. When we were discharged from the hospital, Kaushal's mother helped me care for Samira at home, while Beebo took on small errands like grocery shopping, as I remained bedridden most days. With Kaushal's new position, I finally had the freedom to temporarily quit working and focus on myself and Samira.

Some of my colleagues disapproved of my decision, insisting that true independence meant dedicating your best years to a company—only to be replaced when someone younger and cheaper came along. But I found staying home liberating. Looking after a newborn felt like a full-time job in itself, and while I planned to return to work one day, it wouldn't be anytime soon.

The gifts never stopped. Chocolates, sweets, fruits, and flowers arrived in abundance. We began giving them away to our maid and neighbours. Beebo even took chocolates and flowers to school, claiming he'd give them to girls he liked, hoping they'd reciprocate. I saw no harm in him trying his luck—after all, you miss all the shots you don't take.

Putting himself out there in real life was certainly better than his misguided belief that there were "hot singles in the area" eagerly waiting to date him, as the website ads claimed. He thought they were genuine and once came to me asking for money to chat with what he believed were a hundred women nearby. When I told him it was a scam and refused to pay, he found another app that allowed him to video call women for free. Apparently, one of them messaged that they couldn't talk because their mother was in the other room, but they urged him to strip in front of the camera. Beebo, in his infinite wisdom, complied without hesitation.

It was, of course, a scam. He was blackmailed—threatened with the release of his nude video unless he paid up. He came to me in tears, and I told him flatly that if he paid once, they'd never stop. Fortunately, they didn't get too far with him when they realised Beebo was a broke teenager.

Within weeks, however, the gifts changed from harmless chocolates and flowers to something far more scandalous.

One afternoon, a delivery man arrived at our doorstep with a large tin box of chocolates. When Beebo answered the door, the man refused to hand it over.

"Sorry, kid," he said. "This is for the man or woman of the house only."

I accepted the unusually large box, and the man left with an unsettling smile—one that suggested I should have been expecting it.

Beebo peered over my shoulder as I stared at the unopened box. "If you don't want it, can I take it to school tomorrow?" he asked.

"Sure," I said. "Let me see what kind of chocolate was meant for my hands only."

As I opened the box, my breath caught. Nestled beneath a neatly arranged gold necklace were several thick bundles of cash—easily double Kaushal's annual salary.

Beebo, unfazed, muttered, "So, is Kaushal a millionaire now too? Tom says he gets bundles of cash as gifts all the time because of how important he is."

I shot him a sharp look. "Go to your room."

The moment Beebo left, I called Kaushal. "Who sent this, and what exactly do they want from you?"

Kaushal's voice was tense. "I'll explain when I get home. It's not safe to talk about this over the phone."

I spent the rest of the day pacing, anxiety twisting in my gut. When Kaushal finally arrived in the evening, he sat me down and said, "It's from one of the Road and Transport Ministry's secretaries, Sobhanuddin. But I haven't received anything official that would involve *that* secretary. Either way, I'm returning it tomorrow."

"Thank you, Kaushal," I murmured, relieved.

He placed the box on the bedside table, next to his wallet and keys, so he wouldn't forget in the morning. Wanting to preserve some sense of normalcy, we went to bed pretending nothing had happened. Samira, thankfully, was a nighttime sleeper and did not give us trouble falling asleep. Unlike most Asian parents, we chose to adopt a more Western approach to raising Samira, providing her with her own room—formerly father's—to encourage independence from the start. At night, we kept our bedroom door open so we could hear her if she woke up and cried.

I woke late in the morning to my phone buzzing.

Kaushal's voice was almost panicked. "I'm at the secretary's house. He says that a gold necklace and two bundles of cash are missing. Nida, please tell me you moved them and know where they are."

The blood drained from my face. "I—I didn't touch anything. Give me a few minutes."

Frantically, I searched under the bed, behind the bedside table—nothing. As I knelt on the floor, breathless with worry, I noticed the maid mopping the living room. She always cleaned the bedrooms first before moving on to the rest of the house.

I rushed to her. "Did you see any jewellery or a bundle of money when you were cleaning our room?"

She smiled, almost eerily. "Of course not, madam. Why would there be bundles of cash lying around?"

Her tone didn't sit right with me, but I forced a nod. "If you find anything, please let me know."

Even as I said it, I knew how ridiculous it sounded. That bundle alone would cover her wages for an entire year, the necklace another. If she had found it, she had every reason to keep it—and no reason to tell me.

After half an hour of searching, I gave up. Kaushal called again. "Well? Did you find it?"

"No," I admitted. "Just tell the secretary we'll pay back the missing amount in cash within a day."

I heard Kaushal repeat my words to the person on the other end—probably the secretary. There was a long silence before the secretary's voice cut through:

"That was a gift, Chief Overseer. If you won't accept the gift, then return it. But do not disrespect us by offering us money."

Kaushal didn't respond. I held my breath.

The secretary continued with a casual tone, almost as if he was repeating something that was already implied. "Look, if you can't return the whole package as is, we'll consider that you've accepted our little 'donation.' You should await further instructions on what we hope this donation will get us... in due course."

We had been reeled in—without even technically accepting the bribe.

That night, Kaushal sat with his head in my lap, tears soaking my lap. "This was a mistake," he whispered. "I never should have taken this job. I shouldn't have listened to you."

I felt the weight of his words. It was sort of my fault, as I had encouraged him to leverage his position for stability. But now, we had no idea what they would ask in return.

We also couldn't simply deposit the remaining cash in a bank—it might raise too many red flags. We had never accepted bribes before, and we weren't planning to make a habit out of it from here onward.

So, for now, Kaushal and I bought a pin-code activated safe and locked the remaining money inside. It was meant to be a temporary solution—just until we figured out a way out of this mess.

After putting Samira to sleep, I walked into Beebo's room, where he was playing an online video game on his phone while chatting with his friends over his headset. He was swearing at the opposing players' actions, but the moment he saw me standing in front of him, he cut himself short. Pulling his headset down, he asked, "Did you need something? I'm in the middle of something."

I told him to pause the game because I needed to talk to him.

He looked at me like I had just asked him to do the impossible. "It's an online game. You can't just pause the game for everyone," he said.

I sighed. "Okay, then at least mute the mic. I need to ask you something important."

Beebo looked annoyed but complied. As soon as I saw him hit the mute button, I asked, "Beebo, did you see a necklace and some money in our room this morning before going to school?"

Still focused on his game, he barely paid attention. "What necklace and money?" he asked.

"The ones in the chocolate box," I clarified.

Without looking up, he nonchalantly replied, "Oh yeah, I think I saw the maid walk out of your room with some money. Not sure about the necklace."

I stared at him in shock. "Beebo, you didn't think this was worth mentioning?"

He shrugged. "You didn't ask until now."

I was furious—at both Beebo and the maid—but I decided not to act on impulse. Instead, I turned and walked back to my room, sitting beside Kaushal, who was lying in bed, scrolling through his laptop with a half-defeated expression.

"Beebo said he saw the maid take some money, but he's not sure about the necklace," I told him.

Kaushal looked up from his screen in disbelief. "And he didn't mention this earlier because?"

"There's no point in pressing this further without solid proof," I said. "I'll ask the maid directly tomorrow."

Kaushal sighed. "And you think she'll tell the truth?"

"I don't know," I admitted. "But what other options do we have?"

He nodded. "Do what you think is best."

The next morning at breakfast, with everyone seated at the dining table, I called the maid over. Without hesitation, I confronted her—something Kaushal later pointed out was uncharacteristic of me. "Beebo said he saw you take the money and necklace. I want you to return them."

She looked stunned, her gaze darting from me to Beebo, then to Kaushal's mother, as if expecting her to defend the maid. Finally, she spoke. "The rascal is lying, madam. He was the one who took the money and necklace."

Kaushal, already irritated, asked, "And you chose to stay silent when Nida asked you yesterday? Why?"

The maid hesitated, realising she had just contradicted herself. "Beebo gave me some money and told me to stay quiet," she quickly added.

Beebo shot back immediately, "I did no such thing! Why are you lying?"

This was going nowhere. Kaushal pulled me into our bedroom and said, "The damage is already done, Nida. Unless whoever stole the necklace returns it, there's nothing we can do. We can't even go to the police, but if we push the maid any further and she reports us, we'll be the ones in trouble. I think you should press Beebo for more information. I think he took it."

I don't know why, but I felt defensive. "For better or worse, Beebo is my brother. I won't accuse him without concrete evidence."

Kaushal exhaled. "Then set up some hidden surveillance cameras. We still have that safe with money inside that needs monitoring. We can log in and check on things from time to time until I figure out how to put this money into the banking system without raising any red flags."

He was referring to money laundering, obviously.

But he wasn't wrong.

Without hesitation, I walked out and fired the maid for lying, fully aware of the consequences. Finding help would now be even more difficult, as she would undoubtedly warn others in her community against working for us. People often underestimate the power of word-of-mouth and referrals, assuming that actions alone will speak for themselves. But without someone to vouch for you, even the best work can go unnoticed. Likewise, even the most reasonable employers can struggle to find help after letting go of a disgruntled worker—regardless of who was truly at fault.

I told Beebo we would discuss the issue later, sent everyone off for the day, and then headed to the local electronics market.

Browsing through portable surveillance cameras, I selected discreet models with audio input capabilities and night vision that would blend in well with our existing electrical fixtures and hired a technician to install them. One was mounted to cover our wardrobe, where the safe was hidden, with a wide-angle view of the entire room. Another was placed in the living room, facing the main entrance, and the last one was set up near Samira's crib in her new room—the one that used to be father's before he passed. I ensured the recording devices were well hidden. When Kaushal's mother asked about the man and the devices, I casually told her the man was an electrician fixing faulty wiring.

Once everything was set up, I messaged Kaushal: *Okay, we can log in anytime and check the feed for up to 48 hours before it resets.*

Unlike usual, he didn't respond immediately—probably caught up with work—so I let it be.

...

Over the next few days, I kept asking Beebo about the necklace in different ways, even assuring him that I wouldn't be angry if he had taken it—as long as he returned it. But he stood by his claim that the maid had stolen it and was trying to pin the blame on him. Meanwhile, every night, I would fast-forward through hours of surveillance footage on my phone, scanning for any discrepancies. But nothing ever seemed out of place.

Kaushal eventually came up with a way to clean the money by injecting funds into a struggling local fabric shop. His plan was to gradually show small, layered investments that would briefly yield high profits before the business inevitably returned to a loss—his exit strategy. He had accounted for everything, even paying taxes on the "cleaned" returns to avoid suspicion.

To our surprise, not only did Kaushal execute his plan flawlessly, but the cash injection actually revived the business. I suggested that he keep some investments in the fabric shop to secure a steady, legal share of the profits. Over the following months, as things stabilised, I gradually lost interest in checking the surveillance footage or routinely counting the money in the safe after Kaushal's transactions. After all, only the two of us knew the pin code.

We eventually found another maid after paying a middleman handsomely for the referral. She was consistently late, barely did her job properly, and oversalted everything she cooked. Finding help was easy—finding good help, however, was another story. Kaushal strictly instructed her never to enter our bedroom, leaving the cleaning up to me, which seemed reasonable.

Life began settling into a steady routine. Kaushal was handling the Turag project efficiently, frequently appearing in the media with reporters praising his swift progress. Some even joked that he should run for the next Road and Transport Office election. His public speaking skills improved significantly—almost as good as the scripts I used to write for him—and he seemed increasingly comfortable with media attention.

...

One morning, as I was gathering laundry from each room, I walked into Beebo's to grab the clothes from his basket. As I bent down to pick them up, I noticed a book on his bed titled *How to Be Like Me*, featuring a familiar-looking boy on the cover. I squinted at the name scrawled at the bottom—sure enough, it was Tom the Teenage Millionaire, the online influencer. How had Beebo gotten his hands on this? Had he borrowed it from a friend at school? If so, that meant other kids were buying into this nonsense too.

Curious, I picked up the book and flipped it open but stopped cold at the first page. Inside was a handwritten note: *To my loyal fan, Beebo. From TTM.*

Tom in his videos didn't seem like the kind of person who would just hand out books for free. A sense of unease crept in, but I pushed it aside and finished loading the laundry.

That night, I brought it up with Kaushal.

"Beebo got a book from his favourite influencer, Tom. The guy even signed a note for Beebo."

Kaushal, busy working on his laptop, barely looked up. "Well, that's nice."

I frowned. "From what I've seen, that finance influencer isn't the type to give away books for free."

Kaushal finally looked at me. "So you think Beebo bought it? How would he even make an overseas transaction?"

"I didn't let him use any of my cards," I said. "I even double-checked online to be sure. You wouldn't have happened to buy him that garbage, would you?"

Kaushal chuckled. "Nida, why would I?"

But my suspicion lingered. "Can you check, please? Just to make sure we're not overlooking something?"

He sighed, then closed what he was doing on his computer and logged into his online banking portal. Sure enough, there was a transaction to the U.S. a month ago—matching the exact price of the book on Tom's website.

"Nida, I have no idea what's going on," Kaushal muttered, scrolling through more transactions.

Amid his usual spending, we noticed frequent, small purchases—barely noticeable on their own—of in-game credits. Kaushal had been too busy to catch them. It was obvious: at some point, Beebo had gotten access to Kaushal's card details, stored them on his phone, and had been using it whenever he wanted.

I lost it right then and there. I screamed Beebo's name at the top of my lungs from my room, while Kaushal kept trying to calm me down. Ignoring him, I stormed into Beebo's room, where he was playing on his phone with his friends online.

Without even glancing up, he said, "Just give me a few minutes. I'm almost done with this round."

I wasn't having any of that. Consumed by rage, I marched up, snatched the phone from his hands, and hurled it against the wall. It shattered on impact, the screen now a spiderweb of cracks. Beebo turned to me with a comically confused expression, as if he couldn't comprehend what had just happened.

I pointed at the book still lying on his bed. "Explain how you bought that."

He barely reacted. "A friend at school gave it to me."

I clenched my fists, barely holding in my frustration. "Beebo, we checked the transaction history. You used Kaushal's card."

His eyes widened momentarily before he quickly countered, "What? No!"

I strode over to where his phone had landed, picking it up. Despite the broken glass, the display was still functioning. Sitting beside him, I pulled up the payment options screen, and there it was—the last four digits of Kaushal's card, stored on his account. I turned the phone toward him. "Ready to tell me the truth now?"

The gall of him. He looked me dead in the eyes and shrugged. "Kaushal let me use it once to buy some game credits. It saved itself."

I could feel the heat rising in me. Scrolling through the transaction history, I pointed at the record of the book purchase. Beebo shifted from feigned confusion to a blank, emotionless stare.

"Well, Kaushal is a millionaire, Nida," he said almost as if he was stating a fact. "He didn't even notice the money was gone."

That was it. Something inside me snapped. I dropped the phone and slapped him—hard—across the face, sending him reeling to the side. But I didn't stop there. I kept hitting him as he tumbled onto the bed, my anger boiling over, until Kaushal rushed in and pulled me away.

"It's okay, Nida. Calm down." He held me back, his voice steady but firm.

Beebo sat up, his face swollen, but he barely reacted. It was as if nothing had happened.

"Remove Kaushal's card details. Now," I ordered.

Beebo shrugged. "Sure. But my phone is cracked now. I'll need a new one, please."

I lunged at him again, but Kaushal restrained me and pulled me out of the room, dragging me to our bed. He sat me down and kept talking me down until the fury began to subside.

That night, I deactivated Kaushal's card, ordered him a replacement, and handed him my cards in the meantime, apologising over and over. As we lay in bed, Kaushal kept reassuring me that it wasn't my fault and that it wasn't a big deal.

But it wasn't just about the book.

I was starting to suspect that Beebo had taken the necklace and the money after all.

S amira turned one, and life was slowly stabilising. Sobhanuddin hadn't asked for any favours yet, and Kaushal was making extraordinary progress on the Turag project. Naturally, success breeds enemies in unexpected places. Among them was Kaushal's Regional Manager, who, along with others, constantly sought to undermine his efforts—nitpicking minor mistakes in a colossal project while conveniently ignoring everything he did right. But we knew better than to indulge petty jealousy, and Kaushal kept pushing forward.

With the increasing workload, Kaushal started coming home late, exhausted from the relentless pressure he had taken on. More often than not, he'd return with brown bags filled with bundles of cash—bribes from politicians and media figures eager to erase any trace of their involvement in the Turag project's corrupt past. The irony was that Kaushal had already purged all records; their secrets were long buried. But if people were willing to pay for a job that was already done, why refuse?

He would leave the cash on the bedside table, too drained to care, before collapsing onto the bed in his work clothes. I made it a habit to wake up, sort through the money, and store it safely. Each time, Kaushal would funnel it into a new local business, quietly laundering it as our empire grew—effortlessly, almost unintentionally.

As for Beebo, he was strictly grounded. Outside of school, he wasn't allowed to go anywhere or do anything without permission. We kept Kaushal's wallet in the safe—an inconvenient but necessary precaution. No matter how much Kaushal assured me that Beebo had just been immature, I enforced the rule, making sure to take the wallet out for him before he left for work. Beebo, for the most part, stayed quietly in his room when he was home. He would come out to eat with us and then retreat back inside.

One morning, I received an urgent call from Beebo's school. The principal wanted me to come in immediately. I left Samira playing with Kaushal's mother, who was already exhausted from my daughter's endless energy but wasn't in a position to say no. Not that she could complain—after all, she was the one who had relentlessly pushed Kaushal to have children, like most aging Asian parents who believe their legacy depends on their children having their own.

It always starts with the promise of looking after the grandkids, wrapped in sentiments about their aging bodies and last wishes to play with them. In reality, they can barely keep up, and within a few years, the responsibility inevitably falls back on the mother and father, who are left to deal with both the joys and burdens of raising a child. If emotional blackmail doesn't work, some of our parents resort to comparisons—pointing out neighbours or relatives with large families while conveniently ignoring those raising children alone in terrible conditions.

Kaushal's mother is a lovely woman, no doubt, but she objected to her precious son marrying me before even meeting me, insisting he deserved someone from a more "functional" family. Her stance softened once she actually got to know me, though she was quick to lay down the rules—no funny business before marriage. She also strongly opposed my idea of living together as a trial run, even though it would have put her concerns about my *functionality* to rest. To her, society would see it as disgraceful.

Apparently, in her view, it was more acceptable to marry and divorce within three months than to live together for a year or two before making it official. What she never understood was that certain members of our society will talk no matter what you do. It's best to ignore them—especially when their opinions are rooted in superstition and impractical ideologies.

I walked to Beebo's school—the one I had chosen primarily for its proximity when we all moved in together. Just a few blocks from our home, it saved both time and commuting costs.

When we first took him in, he was six years old and hadn't yet started school, so I enrolled him in one that fit my budget after settling on where to live. At the time, a prestigious school was out of reach, but a few years into work—after Kaushal and I earned promotions in our respective jobs and splitting rent eased the financial strain—I was in a better position to give Beebo more options.

Still, Beebo insisted on staying at his school. He said that it was the only consistent thing in his life, and he didn't want to leave behind his friends. I didn't have the heart to take that away from a child who had already been through so much. After all, it's not the school that makes the students famous—it's the students who make a name for themselves, for better or worse. And Beebo was almost always the latter. He was constantly getting into fights with other boys, and I could only wonder what kind of trouble he had landed himself in this time.

When I arrived at the principal's office, I found another set of parents seated in front of her, their daughter standing beside them. On the opposite side of the room stood Beebo, glaring at the girl with what looked like genuine annoyance.

The principal looked up as I entered. "Ah, Mrs. Nida, please have a seat."

I wasn't sure what was happening, but I shot Beebo a sharp look. He understood and immediately averted his gaze from the girl. I turned to her parents, but they refused to acknowledge me.

The principal introduced me. "This is Nida Oman, Bashir Oman's older sister. She is his legal guardian."

The woman sitting next to me scoffed. "No wonder the boy has no manners. He needed a mother and a proper beating."

My fingers twitched, but I kept my composure. Instead, I turned to the principal. "What did Beebo... I mean, Bashir, do?"

The principal raised an eyebrow. "I don't even know where to start. Let's begin with why we're here today."

I nodded.

"The young lady here is Tanya," she continued. "She's Bashir's senior, and he has been harassing her repeatedly."

Beebo immediately protested, "No, I didn't harass her!"

I turned to him and snapped, "Shut up, Beebo! Let her speak!"

I knew I should have handled it more gracefully in front of the other parents, but I couldn't bring myself to hear another one of his lies.

The principal cleared her throat. "He sent Tanya a very vulgar, albeit slightly odd, message."

Beebo mumbled, "It wasn't me. Elias probably sent it when he took it to the repair shop."

Then it dawned on me—how had I not noticed that Beebo had fixed his phone? He was grounded and never even mentioned it. And where did he get the money for the repair?

The principal tried to ignore Beebo but failed. She continued, "Regardless, the message came from your phone and was sent to Tanya's. It read..." She pulled out a printed screenshot of the conversation and read aloud, "'...send photo of bobs and vagene.'"

Tanya's parents gasped, visibly horrified.

I, on the other hand, was just confused. I leaned in and asked the principal, "I'm sorry, ma'am. What does that mean?"

She gave me a puzzled look, unsure if I was being serious.

Beebo, unable to contain himself, muttered, "Uh... Nida... Elias meant boobs and vagina."

The parents gasped again, the mother nearly fainting.

The principal's face turned red with rage. "Bashir Oman! This is a respectable school, and we do not tolerate such language!"

I wasn't defending Beebo, but my response made it seem that way. "Uh, Principal ma'am... 'vagina' is a scientific word, isn't it? Why are we treating it as taboo?"

The principal was livid. "Mrs. Nida, are you defending Bashir's actions!?"

I realised my mistake. "What? No! I'm not defending that little sh*t."

The principal gasped. "Mrs. Nida, language!"

Tanya's mother chimed in, "The apple doesn't fall far from the tree!"

I immediately apologised for my crude language and refocused. "Look, Principal ma'am, I might have believed you if you'd said my brother sent Tanya a message asking to see her 'boobs and vagina'"—Tanya's mother gasped again on cue, but we all ignored her this time—"but I know my brother. And I know he can spell those words, along with all their synonyms."

The principal hesitated, then nodded. "Yes... he is doing quite well in English. Nevertheless, the message came from his phone, and he must take responsibility."

Beebo turned to Tanya, as if no one else existed in the room. "Tanya, you've known me for a year. Do you really think I'd send you something this crude? I gave you heaps of chocolate and flowers. I took you and your friends out for lunch so many times. Have I ever said anything remotely inappropriate?"

My mind latched onto one particular part of that sentence—*taking her and her friends out for lunch.*

While it was obvious the girl had been stringing him along and milking him for all he was worth, *his* worth shouldn't have let him afford paying for so many mouths. I had made sure of that by strictly rationing his monthly allowance.

I turned to him. "Beebo, where did you get the money for those lunches?"

Before he could answer, Tanya cut in. "That was months ago. We hadn't spoken in ages, and suddenly you send me *this*?" she said pointing to the printed screenshot in the principal's hands.

The room instantly devolved into what felt like a messy divorce trial, with Beebo and Tanya barking at each other while the principal struggled to maintain control.

Beebo snapped, "You stopped replying to my messages the moment I told you I couldn't take you and your friends out anymore because I was grounded."

The principal raised the screenshot again, trying to regain order. "Bashir Oman, it does not matter what led to it. What matters is that you sent a girl a message asking to see her 'bobs and vagene.' This will be recorded in your dismissal report. Our school has a zero-tolerance policy for sexual harassment. Now apologise to Miss Tanya so we can move on to the next matter."

I immediately caught on. "Dismissal report?"

The principal sighed. "We'll get to that, Mrs. Nida. For now, Bashir, apologise."

Beebo locked eyes with Tanya. "I'm sorry, Tanya. I'm sorry that I didn't understand that you weren't interested in me. Tom said that the only way to win a woman over is through expensive gifts and taking her out to dinner."

The principal leaned toward me, whispering, "Who is Tom?"

I whispered back, "The Teenage Millionaire. A social media influencer and financial scammer."

We turned our attention back to Beebo as he continued, "I tried to make the most of what I could offer. I'm sorry I thought you were interested in me when you said you'd go to lunch only if I took all of your friends too."

Tanya nodded, but her mother snapped, "That wasn't even an apology! That was a theatrical monologue!"

I couldn't help myself. I turned to her and said, "Be happy with what you got. He doesn't even give me that!"

The principal quickly stepped in, cutting off the exchange. She stated that Tanya and her parents had received Beebo's apology and politely asked them to leave, as there were several other matters concerning Beebo that she needed to discuss with me. I gulped as Tanya and her parents exited, leaving me alone to face the principal.

"That wasn't all?" I asked hesitantly.

The principal sighed. "That message? No, that was just a small fraction. Tanya's parents were offended and insisted that I address it separately alongside the other issues that will ultimately lead to Bashir's dismissal."

Of course. I should've known. Tanya's parents made generous donations to the school every year. Naturally, the school had to keep them happy.

I turned to Beebo, utterly baffled. "Beebo, what have you done?"

He scoffed. "Nothing that serious. They're blowing things out of proportion."

I barely had time to react before the principal snapped at Beebo, "Quiet!"

She then turned to me, pulling out a thick file and setting it on the desk with a heavy thud. "Nida, these are all the complaints from girls at school that came in against Bashir immediately after Tanya lodged hers."

I stared at the overstuffed file, its pages struggling to stay contained within the binder.

This time, I gasped. "How many girls lodged complaints?"

The principal, puzzled by my question, followed my gaze to the bulging file before responding, "Oh, there were eleven formal complaints. These are printed copies of all the screenshots of the conversations. It also includes printouts of social media posts from other girls—some of them wrote entire essays about how Bashir made them feel, ending with a hashtag: '#MeToo.'"

I frowned. "Wait, isn't that a breach of privacy? How did you even get a hold of these?"

"The girls made the posts public, Mrs. Nida," the principal replied matter-of-factly. "We have a tutor at the school who checks students' social media during her lunch break and reports anything concerning. She came across these posts, brought them to my attention, and we called the girls in to testify and provide proof of the conversations. We wanted to ensure our disciplinary action against Bashir was both strong and fair."

I hesitated. "And then?"

The principal sighed. "The poor girls must be traumatised by what Bashir said to them. Most refused to show the messages. One even claimed they were so distressing she deleted them immediately."

Beebo finally spoke up. "Principal madam, while it's true I messaged several girls, some of the ones who posted those essays online—I've never even spoken to them. They're probably just jumping on the victim bandwagon for attention or sympathy from the teachers."

The principal's face hardened. "Be quiet, Bashir. The nerve you have—to defend yourself and try to blame the victims."

I sighed, listening to their exchange, unsure of what to believe anymore.

"Principal madam, I'm happy for you to detain him for as long as you see fit—make him do community service after school," I offered, hoping for a compromise.

The principal looked at me, almost exasperated. "Mrs. Nida, this isn't about Bashir getting into fights with other kids and ending up worse off. In most of those cases, he got more than he gave."

Beebo, clearly offended, interjected, "I gave them some too!"

The principal dismissed him with a bluntness that had abandoned any pretence of politeness. "Keep telling yourself that, Bashir. Picking fights doesn't make you look strong—it makes you look thick-headed. It's even worse when teachers have to pull you out to save you from getting beaten up, which just makes you look pathetic."

I turned back to the principal, dreading the answer to my next question. "Then what is the punishment?" I silently prayed she wouldn't repeat the word she had mentioned before—*dismissal*.

But that was exactly what she said.

"Mrs. Nida, verbally abusing girls who chose not to respond to his advances, trying to win them over by flaunting thick stacks of cash, and even threatening them when they weren't impressed by his tasteless displays of wealth—these are things we expect from washed-up celebrities facing child support lawsuits, not from schoolchildren."

I thought bitterly to myself—schoolchildren who grow up idolising these very celebrities and mindless social media influencers who glorify wealth and ignorance.

The principal continued in a firm tone. "I'm sorry, Mrs. Nida, but the committee has decided to expel Bashir Oman. This is his dismissal letter, already signed." She slid the document across the table.

I picked it up and read the reason for expulsion: *Multiple counts of sexual abuse and violence against women.*

I felt my breath catch as I looked up. "Principal madam, I have to submit this letter for his next school admission. No school will take him after seeing this reason for dismissal."

The principal's voice was cold. "That is not our problem, Mrs. Nida. You should have raised him better."

My face fell. "Can I see the screenshot where he sent a photo holding the stack of money?"

She sighed. "Which one do you want to see?"

"All of them."

She sifted through the file, pulling out eleven sheets of paper and passing them to me. I stared at the screenshots, each conversation painfully similar.

Beebo would begin with a cringeworthy, unsolicited "Hi gorgeous." When the girls ignored him, he would follow up with a photo of himself holding a stack of cash, captioned: "I can show you a good time!" And when they still didn't respond, he would resort to insults, badmouthing them in every way imaginable.

As I flipped through the pages in horror, Beebo piped up confidently, "Nida, Tom said to be assertive. That women look for wealth, and if they don't respond, it means they think you're poor or ugly. In that case, you have to be assertive and show them who's boss!"

The principal scoffed, as she used sarcasm to respond to Beebo. "Well, aren't you a Prince Charming? I can't imagine why girls try to stay as far away from you as possible."

I didn't respond. I just kept shuffling through the images—sealed bundles, bank tags, the same predictable pattern. Then, as I reached the oldest screenshot my hands froze.

It was from a year ago. The picture showed a familiar stack of cash in Beebo's hands. There was his bed in the background, and on it was unmistakably the gold necklace!

Goosebumps prickled my skin.

I almost lost it right then and there. I lunged at Beebo, my fists landing blow after blow, slapping and beating him until his lean body crumpled to the ground. The principal didn't even try to stop me.

"Where is the necklace, you little sh*t?!" I screamed, my hands pounding against him.

Beebo finally lashed back, gasping through gritted teeth, "I gave it to Tanya! The b*tch conveniently left that part out when she lodged a complaint."

I froze as my breath remained ragged. Slowly, I turned to the principal, expecting her to intervene before I even spoke. She did.

"I'm not going to ask a victim of sexual violence to come back in here, especially after Bashir used such language to describe her!" she said firmly.

"Principal madam, please," I pleaded, my voice quieter but no less desperate. "At least let me speak to her. That necklace was very important to my family—we thought it was stolen."

The principal sighed, then motioned for Beebo to wait in her office as she led me down the hallway to Tanya's classroom. I stood outside as she stepped in, returning a moment later with the girl in tow.

I faced Tanya, my voice calmer but insistent. "Look, Tanya, I know my brother is an a**hole. But that necklace means a lot to me. If Beebo gave it to you, please... just give it back."

Tanya remained silent—not as if she didn't know what I was talking about, but as if she were deciding how to respond. After a moment, she finally said, "Mrs. Nida, I don't know what you're talking about. Now, can I go back to class?"

I started to stop her, but the principal intervened. "Mrs. Nida, if you want to pursue this further, I suggest you go through official channels. File a police report and disclose the details of the necklace. They can investigate." Her voice was firm. "I'm afraid I can't entertain this any further."

I knew that wasn't an option. Kaushal's friend, the Chief of Dhaka Police, had warned against involving law enforcement in anything related to 'unofficial donations.' Calling the police would be catastrophic. It wouldn't just be about the necklace—it would unleash a Pandora's box of scrutiny. The Chief Overseer of the Turag Project—now practically a celebrity—caught accepting bribes and falsifying documents? The media would have a field day. No outlet would pass up a scandal like that.

I relented.

Back in the principal's office, Beebo sat on the floor, blood dripping from his nose. At some point, one of my blows must have injured him. He clutched his face, trying to contain the bleeding, but I didn't care.

I snatched the dismissal letter off the desk and walked out. "Come on," I ordered. Beebo wordlessly followed.

When we arrived home, Beebo moved silently toward his room, but I stopped him at the door.

"Where's the rest of the money, you little sh*t?"

He turned to face me, his expression blank. He didn't answer.

I lost it again. My hands came down on him, striking him over and over. In hindsight, he could have fought back—he could have defended himself—but he didn't.

After a few blows, he finally relented. "Okay, okay! I don't have it anymore! I'll tell you what happened, just please stop hitting me."

I caught my breath, my hands still shaking, and dragged him to the dining table. I sat across from him, staring him down.

"Go on," I said. "Let's hear it."

Beebo sighed and muttered, "Okay, I invested it all in a business—just like Tom said would make me a millionaire and become a celebrity just like Kaushal."

I narrowed my eyes in annoyance. "What business?"

Beebo straightened up as best he could while clutching onto his nose. It was as if he was getting ready to impress me with his genius. "Well, I got an email from an overseas investor. They had an incredible business opportunity, and I knew immediately it would be my big break—Tom always talks about how important people always reach out via emails in his videos! The person who reached out to me said they owned a silver mine in Africa that needed repairs after a recent earthquake. They were selecting 20 people at random to become investors, and I was one of them."

I stared at Beebo, unsure if he was lying again or if he was genuinely this... stupid.

Oblivious to my disbelief, he continued, "I replied right away, just like Tom says—you never pass up an opportunity! I told them I was interested. Then they asked how much I was willing to invest, and I remembered Tom saying, 'The more you invest, the more you make.' So, I counted all the money I had and offered them everything. But I made sure to mention that I didn't have a credit card, just cash."

I had to pause. "Beebo, why did you steal from us? Why not just tell me you wanted to start your own business?"

Beebo gestured toward his swollen, broken nose, still pressing an ice pack to it. "Because you don't listen. You just jump to conclusions."

As infuriating as that was, I motioned for him to continue. "Fine. What happened next?"

He brightened up, as if his story was going perfectly. "They told me I didn't need a credit card. I just had to buy gift cards from local supermarkets in the amount I wanted to invest and email them the gift card numbers."

I facepalmed. "Tell me you didn't."

"I did!" Beebo nodded proudly. "I skipped school one day, went to every supermarket I could find, and bought as many gift cards as I could with the money."

I clenched my jaw. Of course, no shopkeeper at a corporate franchise would find it suspicious that a kid was bulk-buying gift cards. As long as the transaction went through, they couldn't care less.

Beebo was still talking. "Then I sent all the gift card numbers via email. It took hours, but I know good things take time! The person on the other end replied almost immediately and said they'd be in touch once the mine was up and running again. It could take a while, but it's totally worth it."

I buried my face in my hands. "Beebo. You didn't think—*not once*—why a big company would reach out to a random teenager in South Asia and ask for *gift cards* as an investment?"

Beebo shrugged. "No. That's how opportunities come. That's how you become a millionaire."

I sighed. He was completely oblivious to the scam he had fallen for. Clearly, Tom the Teenage Millionaire never warned about scammers—probably because he was one himself.

"Beebo, that was a *Nigerian Prince scam*," I said slowly, enunciating every word. "You are *never* getting anything in return."

Beebo scoffed, as if *I* were the clueless one. "You don't understand business, Nida! I'm sure Kaushal would've appreciated it. *He's* the successful one, not you."

At that point, I didn't have the energy to argue. I took a deep breath and asked instead, "Beebo, how did you even get hold of the money?"

He answered bluntly, "I asked Kaushal for some when he came back from work with a brown bag, and he'd hand me a bundle from it."

I stared at him, knowing full well he was lying. But I didn't have the energy to deal with him anymore.

I sent Beebo back to his room, deciding to talk to Kaushal when he got back. As I sat in my room, feeding Samira in my lap, I remembered that Kaushal had come in with a brown bag two nights ago. The footage should still be in the system. I loaded it up on my phone, which showed the last log in was five months ago. I scrolled through the reels from that night as Samira happily ate small cut fruits from a bowl on my lap.

I fast-forwarded through the footage, watching as I slept in my room and Samira rested peacefully in her crib in the other room. The front door opened, and Kaushal walked in with his brown bag. As he approached our room, I slowed the footage down. Beebo's door creaked open just enough for him to peek out before quickly closing it again. I fast-forwarded again, watching Kaushal place the bag, along with the rest of his belongings, on the bedside table before heading into the bathroom. I remained asleep the entire time.

Moments later, Beebo's door opened. He rushed across the living room and, as I switched to the footage in our room, I saw him tiptoe in, open the brown bag, and swipe a bundle of cash. He paced back to his room and quietly shut the door behind him. It seemed like he had been doing this every time Kaushal brought in a bag of bribe money.

Kaushal came out of the bathroom, collapsed onto the bed in his work clothes, and the jostling of the bed woke me. I quickly went through my usual routine of sorting the cash into the safe, unaware that Beebo had been swiping it during that brief window.

Now, knowing I had him on tape, I faced a dilemma: I couldn't let Beebo know we had evidence, or he'd become more cautious and harder to catch. But I also couldn't let him keep stealing, even if it was bribe money. I decided to stay quiet until Kaushal came home that night, which, as usual, was late.

I stayed up, hoping to discuss the matter with him while the memory was fresh. As he walked into the room, tired, I didn't waste any time showing him the recording I had downloaded before it was erased.

Kaushal seemed indifferent. "It's not our money to begin with. Let's not bother about it."

I snapped back, "I will not raise a thief in this house, Kaushal. I don't want Samira to pick up Beebo's values."

Kaushal, confused, replied, "If you're struggling to keep Beebo in check, have you considered sending him away to a boarding school to straighten him out?"

I responded, "Yeah, that's not an option anymore. He was dismissed from school today for sexual violence toward women."

Kaushal, unfazed, suggested, "I could pull some strings to get him into a good one for all boys. We can give the school a sizeable donation to turn a blind eye."

I retorted quickly, "Then when he gets out, he'll be a sex-crazed pervert and turn into a serial killer who assaults women!"

Kaushal chuckled. "That's a bit dramatic, isn't it? I'm from an all-boys school too. Does that make me a pervert?"

I shot him a pointed look. "Kaushal, you and Beebo weren't born into the same circumstances."

Kaushal sighed, clearly frustrated. "Okay, clearly you're not expecting a solution from me, so tell me what you want to do, and I'll listen and nod accordingly."

I stared at him bluntly. "I don't want you bringing any bribe money back to this house. To be honest, I'm still shocked that people are still offering you money to have their shady records wiped from the project."

Kaushal paused, likely calculating his response. "The last few payments weren't from former associates to the project; they were donations to lobby certain contractors to supply logistics and materials for the project."

I was taken aback. "Kaushal, we didn't discuss this. I didn't agree to this."

He reassured me, "Nida, the suppliers were already on my shortlist. It didn't hurt to take some payment to move them up the queue."

I pushed, "But Kaushal, when will it be that someone pays you to lobby for something that damages the project or your reputation more than the immediate benefits?"

Kaushal spoke slowly, "Nida, we own enough local businesses to not raise any red flags if we start laundering more money through other fronts. Besides, I won't accept bribes for anything that damages the Turag project."

I nodded, still feeling uneasy, and slightly betrayed that he was withholding information. I should have seen it coming—it's never just "that one payout, and we're done." Human desires and greed go hand in hand when left unchecked.

I continued, "Don't bring bribe money back to the house. Keep it in your office until the end of the week, and we'll go together and put it in whatever business you think is appropriate."

Kaushal agreed. "That's fine. But don't worry, Nida. I don't want to bother you with the investments. I have a good grip on how the system works and how to work my way around it."

While it felt like he was cutting me out of the process, I had asked for it, and I knew it was more important to keep the peace at home than worry about where the money was going. After all, the clean profits were still coming back home.

Kaushal tried to lighten the mood by leaning in close to kiss me, making an evident attempt to be intimate. But I felt nothing now, just as I had the last time he made advances, or the time before that. Ever since he took up the Turag Project, I had felt a disconnect. As always, I pushed him aside and gave the most clichéd excuse known to womankind: "I'm tired and have a headache. I need to sleep."

Kaushal didn't push, just walked to the closet, changed clothes, and climbed into bed beside me and switched the bedside lamp off.

As I lay in bed, facing the other way, Kaushal's arms wrapped around me, trying to pull me closer into his embrace. That's when I spoke up. "I don't ever want you to withhold information from me again."

At that, he released his hold and simply replied, "Okay," before turning over to the other side of the bed.

I wasn't going to make some dramatic threat about leaving him if he didn't start sharing things with me. No couple needs to tell each other everything, and from what I've seen with my now-divorced ex-colleagues, constantly threatening to leave over anything—big or small—can often be a sign that the person was looking for an excuse to end things anyway. I had no intentions of leaving Kaushal, especially after everything he'd done to look after father and now my kleptomaniac little brother.

For some reason, this didn't feel like the "happily ever after" I had once dreamed of as a child when I played with Barbie dolls and pasted Barbie stickers everywhere.

Nida | Chapter 6. Live and let live

Samira turned three. I started hiring a host of home tutors to homeschool Beebo, as getting him admitted to any nearby school was impossible—even with a sizeable donation. The schools feared for their reputation and the potential risk he posed to the daughters of influential individuals more than they valued any amount of money I could offer. It seemed that money couldn't buy goodwill when the scandal attached to it was far more damaging to business than the bribe was beneficial.

Samira adored Beebo, often sitting on his lap for hours while he read her favourite stories. It felt almost wholesome—watching them from the couch on lazy afternoons—until Kaushal's mother inevitably interrupted the moment with some absurd news she'd found on social media, complete with obviously doctored images she believed to be legitimate. She would frequently forward them to me, urging me to share them with everyone I knew, just as she did with her own contacts to "spread the truth." No amount of explanation could convince her of what fake news looked like or how deceptive it could be.

Kaushal had given her a debit card, which he periodically topped up with small amounts. She would then go on to spend it on hilariously bad "deals" online, like 99% off designer products that never arrived. Kaushal had set up the card to notify him whenever she attempted a sketchy purchase, allowing him to decline the transaction before any money was lost. Truth be told, I suspected she relied on him to filter out her reckless spending rather than genuinely trying to be careful.

To keep Beebo occupied and give him a sense of responsibility, I allowed him to leave the house in the morning for groceries and in the afternoon to meet his local friends—though he had to be back within two hours. With no more bundles of cash lying around and our cards locked in a safe while we were home, there wasn't much left for him to steal. I periodically checked the surveillance footage to see if he was up to anything late at night, and while he would still peek out of his room when Kaushal came home, he no longer saw a bag in his hands. That, perhaps, was why he had stopped sneaking into our room.

Still, I remained paranoid. I kept track of every loose bit of cash and started maintaining an inventory of all valuables in the house. I rushed to the door whenever deliveries arrived, uncertain of what they might contain. In hindsight, I should have accepted defeat and sent Beebo to a military boarding school to straighten him out. But I couldn't bring myself to do it—I truly believed he deserved better than the life our father had put him through.

I never liked the company he kept. His friends looked like street thugs, and while I made it clear they were never welcome in our home, I didn't completely forbid him from associating with them. Maybe I was misjudging them, the way I had initially misjudged Sufi, Shiro, and Rajesh.

But the more I let things slide, the worse it seemed to get. More recently, I began catching him on surveillance again, snooping around the house at night while Kaushal and I slept. He would slip into our room, walking around as if searching for cash or cards. I decided not to tell Kaushal—if he found out, he would push harder for sending Beebo away, and I wasn't ready for that. Not that I was handling things particularly well myself.

The late-night prowling became more frequent and blatant. I started to worry that one night he would wake Kaushal up, and things would spiral completely out of my control. So, I decided to set up a sting operation to catch him in the act without revealing that I had hidden cameras monitoring him.

One afternoon, after Beebo's tutor left and Samira ran into his room, I took advantage of his open door. I placed a bundle of cash and a brown bag filled with waste paper on the bedside table and walked away to the bathroom. From there, I logged into the surveillance system on my phone. Sure enough, Beebo began eyeing the bag as he played with Samira around the house, repeatedly walking past the room and sneaking glances at it. The cash outside the bag was surely enough to pique his interest.

That night, I left our bedroom door completely open and made sure the brown bag was still visible on the bedside table. Kaushal noticed and asked about it, but I only told him I'd explain later. He didn't press further—he probably had a long day and didn't have the energy for my antics.

I lay on my side with my phone charging, the surveillance feed running. Tucking it between my pillow and blanket to keep it out of sight, I cycled between the three different camera feeds, waiting. Five hours passed. My eyes were about to shut when, at the very edge of the screen, I saw a shadow shift near the doorway.

Switching to the living room feed, I saw Beebo—barefoot, tiptoeing toward our room.

I quickly turned my phone screen off and waited a few more seconds. As he reached for the brown bag and I heard his fingers brushing against it, I sat up abruptly. His eyes widened in pure shock, caught red-handed as I stared him down.

Silently, I raised a finger to my lips, signalling him to stay quiet so as not to wake Kaushal. Then, with a nod, I gestured for him to step outside. He obeyed.

Once in the living room, I motioned for him to sit down.

I would have preferred to start beating him up, but that would make too much noise—and I wanted answers first.

"Beebo, what on earth do you think you were doing?"

He remained silent, likely realising that lying his way out of this wasn't an option. After what felt like an eternity, he finally whispered, "I owe Elias and his boys some money, Nida. Every time we meet, he keeps asking for it, and I don't have anything. My investment in the silver mines hasn't turned up a profit yet."

I let out a deep sigh. "Beebo, of course nothing is going to turn up. You were scammed. Now tell me—what exactly do you owe Elias for?"

Beebo didn't hesitate. "Well, it started with non-fungible tokens... or NFTs."

I had no idea what that meant until he explained it—some nonsense about owning digital paintings, but only one copy of each existed, making them rare. Apparently, with the right marketing, their prices were supposed to skyrocket, making them a great investment. That was the theory. In reality, very few people made money off them, let alone turned a profit.

"And what exactly happened?" I asked.

"Elias and his boys didn't know anything about NFTs, so I told them they were the future. I convinced them that if they invested early, they could make a fortune."

I stared at him, dumbfounded. "Beebo, that's financial advice! You don't tell people what to do with their money!"

But he remained firm. "It was supposed to be foolproof! Tom said NFTs were going to blow up, and that we should jump onto his marketplace while prices were still discounted."

I buried my face in my hands. "Beebo, you idiot. Your 'influencer' was marketing his own products, and you dragged other people into it. What happened next?"

"I got Elias and his boys to buy a few NFTs, whatever profits they would make, I wanted 6% of the cut. But after a few weeks, the website was taken down, and the price of the tokens plummeted. Now they wanted *me* to pay them back because they blame me for their losses. As if I forced them to buy it!" Beebo shrugged, feigning innocence, as though he was being unfairly accused.

I shook my head. "People will always blame you if your advice loses them money, but if it works out, they'll take credit for being brave and adventurous. What were you thinking? Your favourite influencer is a scammer!"

Beebo ignored my comment and continued, "It was unfortunate that the NFTs didn't work out, so I tried to make it right. I found a better way to get their money back—plus more—if they invested a little extra. There was this new cryptocurrency called Rocket Coin that was picking up steam. I told them if they bought in, they could sell in a few weeks and make all their money back—and then some."

I stared at him, stunned. "Beebo, you just ran a Reload Scam without even realising it. You played into Elias's desperation to recoup his loss and gave him another bad investment to chase."

Beebo shrugged. "Fancy words. Well, Elias and the boys listened, bought some Rocket Coins, sold them after a month, and made back everything—plus more!" He grinned, almost proud of his accidental financial advice.

I frowned. "Beebo, you just got lucky." But something wasn't adding up. "If they made their money back, why do you still owe them?"

Beebo's voice dropped. "After making a profit, they dumped everything they had into Rocket Coin... and it tanked overnight. They lost everything."

I sighed. "Beebo, that's on them. They took the risk."

Beebo shook his head. "Yeah, but they blame me for introducing them to the idea."

"That makes no sense!" I exclaimed. But then I caught myself and asked, "Beebo... what do they want now?"

He let out a deep sigh. "They told me I have to show up and face them every afternoon until I help them recover *all* of their money. Or else..."

I braced myself, expecting some vague threat to his life. But his next words were worse.

"Or else they'll come to our home and do terrible things to you and Samira."

The blood drained from my face. Beebo wasn't just in trouble—he had dragged all of us into it. If Kaushal found out thugs were threatening Samira, I wasn't sure how he would react. And I wasn't willing to find out.

I made my decision instantly. "How much do they think you owe them?"

Beebo told me the number. In the past, it might have been a staggering amount, but with our growing empire, it was manageable—barely an inconvenience.

"Fine," I said. "I'll go with you next time and pay them off. I don't trust you to handle it." I fixed him with a hard stare. "After that, you stay away from these guys. No more deals. No more scams. Nothing."

It wasn't the choice I wanted to make. But given the situation, it was the only one I had.

...

The next afternoon, I left Samira with Kaushal's mother and walked with Beebo to the roadside tea stall where he usually met Elias. I should have told Kaushal and brought backup, but I was terrified of what he'd ask me to do next—like sending Beebo away immediately to a boarding school.

Five motorcycles were parked nearby, and a group of middle-aged men, varying in build, were making noise at the stall. As we approached, one of them nudged another, who was drinking tea and eating bread. Upon seeing us, the man set his food aside and stepped forward.

He wore a t-shirt, ripped jeans, and sandals that exposed his long, filthy toenails. His hair was slicked back with too much gel, and he sported a thin moustache. He grinned.

"Beebo! I see you brought company." He extended a hand toward me, his pinky nail grown long and caked with dirt.

Beebo quickly spoke up. "This is my sister, Nida."

I ignored the handshake. "You Elias?"

He nodded. "Yes, I am. Pleasure to meet you, ma'am."

I cut straight to the point. "Why do you think Beebo owes you?"

Elias glanced back at his friends before bursting into laughter. "Why wouldn't he? He told us to invest in Rocket Coin, we did, and we lost a lot of money. It's only fair that he pays us back."

I folded my arms. "Beebo said you made your money back the first time, right?"

He nodded. "That's why we invested again."

I held his gaze. "There was no guarantee that past performance would predict future results. You took a risk, and it didn't work out. Why blame someone else for the risks you chose to take?"

Elias stepped closer, but I didn't move. "Because, Beebo's sister, I don't like losing." His voice was low, deliberate. "I'm the local leader of the political student league, and I always come out on top."

He looked far too old to be a student—probably in his mid-thirties. I took a step back, paritally out of fear, but also to assess my next move. "How much do you *think* Beebo owes you?"

Elias smirked. "I *know* exactly how much he owes me." He named the same amount Beebo had told me—the amount I had in an envelope tucked inside my handbag.

I pressed on. "And is that why you keep calling him here every afternoon?"

Elias scoffed. "He needs to know his place, Beebo's sister." Then, as if to make his point clearer, he pulled a pistol from behind his back and casually waved it around. "I've put people down for much less money. I'm sure Beebo told you what I said I'd do to his little niece."

I would be lying if I said I wasn't scared. But I refused to let him see it.

I reached into my bag, pulled out the envelope, and handed it to him. "The full amount you claim he owes you is in there. This is the last time he's coming to see you. Anything else you do is on you—you don't blame Beebo, and you stay far away from us."

Elias peeked inside and smirked sarcastically before tossing the envelope to one of the boys on a motorcycle. "Count it."

The guy counted quickly and nodded.

Elias grinned. "Well, Beebo's sister, I suppose all debts are settled."

I grabbed Beebo's arm and pulled him away. "I never want to see you anywhere near Beebo or my family again."

As we walked off, I leaned toward Beebo and whispered, "This is the last time you're leaving the house to make friends until you finish home schooling and leave permanently for university."

Beebo stumbled. "Leave permanently?"

"Yes. Find your own footing and do your own thing. I'll pay for your university, but I'm done covering for you. I'm done lying to Kaushal."

I knew I was making myself a hypocrite. I had demanded Kaushal tell me everything, yet here I was, keeping one of the most dangerous moments of Beebo's life a secret from him.

...

A few weeks passed, and the only time Beebo left home was with me for groceries. I didn't let him go out alone and kept him under constant supervision, which on its own was exhausting. Meanwhile, Kaushal started coming home later than usual and barely replied to my texts while at work. When he did come home, he played with Samira for a bit, exchanged small talk with me, and went straight to bed. He stopped mentioning the Turag Project altogether.

One night, as we lay in bed, Kaushal finally spoke. "I have to travel interstate for a few weeks starting next week to sort out a shipment for the project. The workers at the metal foundry have unionised and are refusing to work, arguing that they do physically harder labour than I do as Chief Overseer yet earn less than 2% of my salary. In response, the board fired everyone in the union and has now tasked me with making alternate arrangements."

He was opening up and I felt like this would be a good way to restart communicating like we used to. I turned around to face him, and asked excitedly, "What's else is going on with the Turag Project? What's new?"

He quickly shut me down, "It'd rather not talk about it."

I took the hint, but still wanted to talk, about anything. "When did the union thing happen?"

"Yesterday," he replied in a single word.

I hesitated before offering, "Do you need any help? Samira and I could join you since it's for a few weeks."

He shut that down too. "No, that won't be necessary, Nida. I have it covered."

I pushed a little. "Alright, but if you need anything—"

He cut me off. "I'll let you know. Thanks, Nida. I need to sleep now. Busy day tomorrow." He rolled over, ending the conversation.

By this point, Beebo and his actions had already planted a seed of paranoia in my mind. Now, it began creeping into everything.

The next night, unable to shake my unease, I called Kaushal around ten. "Hey, do you want me to make you something special for dinner?"

"No, thanks," he said. "I'll eat before I leave the office, like always. You should go to bed."

I wasn't asking because of dinner. I was asking to put my restless mind at ease. "You're in the office?" I pressed.

There was a pause before he answered. "Yes."

"Okay then. See you soon." I ended the call.

Something felt off. My instincts were screaming at me, so I pulled up the car tracking app. His car wasn't near his office—it was on the move. I watched the screen as it blipped across the map, heading to the other side of the city before stopping at a club called the Watering Hole.

That club was notorious. It attracted all kinds—drug addicts, escorts, and people looking for trouble.

My mind raced through every possibility. I stared at the tracking screen, fixated on that small blip for an hour, until it finally moved again—this time, heading home. I checked the travel history. Kaushal had been driving to the Watering Hole once a week. Sometimes twice.

Whatever he was doing there, he wasn't telling me, like everything else he had going on in his life outside of home.

I started losing sense of time as I stared blankly at the GPS blips until I snapped out and noticed the car was in our driveway. I closed the app just as the front door opened. Kaushal walked in, pretending as if he had come straight from work. I said nothing. Maybe this was karma for hiding the truth about Beebo and Elias from him.

The day Kaushal left for his trip, his mother also packed up to visit her sister in Sylhet, leaving only me, Samira, and Beebo at home. It wasn't unusual for his mother—she often visited family around the country and enjoyed her retirement. But it didn't stop the sinking feeling in my chest.

I didn't know how to explain it. The paranoia of having Beebo at home *and* the uncertainty of what Kaushal was really up to. That night, I woke up to an empty bed, my chest aching from the weight of my thoughts. I went over to Samira's room and stood over her toddler bed for hours, watching her sleep, as if making sure she was still there. I realised I was losing my sense of time, drifting into my thoughts for hours without even noticing.

When I realised the irrational and downright creepy things that I was doing, I decided I needed a change of pace.

On the second day after Kaushal left, I handed Beebo some money and told him, "I'm taking Samira somewhere for a few days. Maybe a resort. Just to clear my head. There's food in the fridge, and you have my permission to go to the groceries *only* if it's absolutely necessary."

I didn't want to leave him alone, but I was suffocating with all the thoughts swirling in my mind. Taking him along would just mean taking a big part of my problem with me on vacation.

But even after arriving at the resort, sitting by the children's pool as Samira played in the water, I still couldn't get my mind to settle down.

A few hours later, I gave up. I packed our bags, called a taxi, and went home.

We arrived late at night. As I walked in, Beebo stepped out of his room, surprised. "I thought you'd be gone for longer. Is everything okay?"

I forced a small smile. "Yeah, I just didn't feel like it anymore."

I took Samira to the bathroom, cleaned her up, and put her to bed in her room. Then, I returned to my room, closed the door behind me, and sighed.

Exhausted, not physically, but mentally, I collapsed onto the bed and let sleep take me.

...

As usual, I woke up in the middle of the night, unable to sleep any longer. Exhausted yet restless, I sat up in bed, only to hear faint whispers coming from the other side of my door. With my door closed, I couldn't make out the words—only that there were voices on the other side. It didn't make sense. My heart pounded as I grabbed my phone and logged into the surveillance feed of the living room. Nothing.

I shook my head, thinking my mind was playing tricks on me, but then I switched over to Samira's room—and my blood ran cold.

Several men—some leaning against the wall, others squatting on the floor. One smoked near the open window while Samira slept in her bed. Beebo stood among them, next to a familiar-looking man casually puffing on a cigarette. My fingers trembled as I zoomed in on the feed, and that's when I saw it—the long nail on the pinky finger holding the cigarette. Elias.

I quickly turned on the audio.

Elias exhaled smoke before replying "You told us the house would be empty for a few days, Beebo. Were you lying to us?".

Beebo coughed in Elias's smoke before speaking back, "She said so herself. How was I supposed to know she'd be back so soon?"

Elias's voice sounded irritated, "You have an annoying habit of overpromising, Beebo."

"I told you I could get your money back, didn't I? Didn't I deliver?" Beebo retored.

Elias responded, "Don't try to sound smart, Beebo. Your sister paid us off not you"

Elias muttered something inaudible, but the last part came through clearly: "We can't do the weapons deal here with your sister and the kid around. You just wasted our time, Beebo, and now you owe us."

My stomach churned and my heart pounded in my chest. Weapons deal?

Panic surged through me. With shaky hands, I slipped on my headphones and called Kaushal. The phone rang for what felt like forever before he finally answered, groggy.

"There are strangers in the house, in Samira's room," I whispered, my voice breaking. "I don't know what to do."

"Is Samira okay?" His voice sharpened.

"She's still asleep. They're just...smoking cigarettes around her." I should have told him about Beebo, but I didn't.

"Stay in your room," Kaushal instructed. "I'll make a call."

A minute later, he called back. "I just spoke to Alaul Uncle; he is personally on his way with his units. Just keep watching—" His voice suddenly cut off.

I frowned. "Kaushal?"

Then, a notification popped up on the surveillance app. *Another user has logged into the feed.*

Kaushal's voice came back. "Why is Beebo standing with them? Nida, what the hell is going on?"

I knew my hearing wasn't the best, and I couldn't always tell if my whispers were louder than they should be. So, I rushed into the bathroom, locked the door, and, between gasping sobs, told him everything—Elias, the threats, the money.

Kaushal listened in silence before saying, "We need to talk. I'll be on the next flight back."

He hung up, but I saw his name remain on the surveillance feed. He was still watching.

Then, I watched on my screen as Elias turned toward Samira.

"Such a pretty little thing," he murmured, exhaling smoke over her face.

The smoke stirred Samira up in her sleep as she began coughing.

Beebo tensed. "Elias, don't do that."

Elias smirked, almost taking Beebo's words of caution as a challenge to his authority. He leaned in closer to Samira. This time, he blew a full mouthful of smoke directly at her. Samira jolted awake, choking violently.

Something inside me snapped.

I dropped my phone and bolted out of my room, screaming, "Get away from her!" like a madwoman.

Elias turned, looking a mix of surprised and amused. "Come now, Beebo's sister. Do you really think it's wise to yell at so many armed men when you're all alone?"

I shoved past them, grabbing Samira from her bed as she coughed into my chest. As I backtracked out of the room, one of the men stepped in front of the door, blocking my exit.

Elias sighed. "You're becoming a real inconvenience, Beebo's sister. We had a deadline to move a shipment of weapons into the university dorms by tomorrow while the guards were paid to look the other way. Now, you've left us with two options—either you take your daughter, stay in your room, and let us finish the deal so Beebo gets his cut, or you compensate us for the trouble you've caused... double what you paid last time!"

Adrenaline drowned out my fear. I clutched Samira tighter, "I'm not letting you do anything in this home *and* I don't owe you sh*t. Get out of my house." Then glaring at Beebo, I continued "...and take that piece of sh*t with you."

Laughter rippled through the group as they closed in. Elias smirked. "Sounds like you chose the second option, Beebo's sister." Then he paused to think, "I have a better idea. How about you show me your 'bobs and vagene' and I will give you a discount on what you owe us?"

Beebo kept his gaze fixed out the window, refusing to look at me as he mumbled, "Elias, let her go. She has nothing to do with this."

Before Elias could respond, the distant wail of sirens cut through the night, growing louder by the second. The flashing red and blue lights reflected against the walls as the police cars screeched to a halt in our driveway. Then, a commanding voice rang out, "This is the police."

Elias groaned in frustration. "Now, now... is that how you treat guests?"

In moments, a loud knock echoed from the front door.

The man blocking my exit stepped aside, and I ran out of Samira's room with my child in my arms to the main door, throwing it open.

Chief inspector of Dhaka Police, Alaul Mofiz, stood there, fifteen officers behind him. "Where are they?"

I pointed toward Samira's room. The police strode in, as Alaul guided me back to my room, "Wait right here, Nida."

He then walked out of the bedroom. I quickly turned on the surveillance feed and I saw him speak briefly with Beebo in the other room before escorting the men out—not in handcuffs, just calmly walking them away.

Samira and I waited in my room as the men headed out the main door.

Once the footsteps settled down, Alaul knocked on my door. I opened the door and stared at him expectantly.

Alaul sighed and said, "Nida, this doesn't qualify as breaking and entering. Your brother invited them in. I can't even press charges since there are no firearms on the premises—looks like the seller never showed up."

I gaped at him. "Are you kidding me? Those men should be behind bars!"

The Chief Inspector exhaled sharply. "Elias is an important figure in the ruling party's student politics and a local leader of the student league. If we arrest him without concrete evidence, we'll have higher-ups breathing down our necks, cutting funds to the station until we're forced to let him go."

I felt helpless. "That means he will come back again and finish what he started!"

Alaul nodded, "No. I told him who your husband is, he should leave you alone now."

I wanted to scream.

This wasn't justice.

As I heard the roar of several motorcycles revving up outside, I realised Elias and his men were about to leave. I walked out to the main door with Samira and found Alaul standing on our porch, saying something to Elias, who turned to give me a sly smile.

Beebo shuffled up beside me. "Nida, I'm sorry, they made me—"

I cut him off mid-sentence. "Not another word."

Grabbing him by the collar, I dragged him outside and shoved him toward Elias. Instead of catching him, Elias simply deflected Beebo aside, letting him stumble and fall to the ground.

"Take this piece of sh*t with you," I spat. "You said he owes you? Make him work for it. But stay away from me and my family."

Elias studied me for a moment, before breaking into an unapologetic smile. "My apologies, Mrs. Veni. Beebo never mentioned who your husband was. Forget what your family owes us."

I thought to myself, "Mrs. Veni?" Kaushal had never insisted I take his surname, always emphasising that I should hold onto my own identity unless I chose otherwise.

I snapped back. "No. A debt is a debt, right? Twice as much? Make Beebo pay for it!"

Alaul stepped in. "Nida, please. I understand you're angry, but this isn't—"

I cut him off too, my voice rising into an incoherent scream, "please leave us alone!" Alaul hesitated before finally gesturing for Elias to take Beebo.

Elias grabbed Beebo by the neck, hoisting him up as Beebo started sobbing. "Nida, please, I'm sorry! Don't do this to me!"

Elias chuckled. "Come, little Beebo. Welcome to the student league. I'm sure we'll find some use for you—until your sister changes her mind and takes you back."

"That will not happen," I hissed.

Alaul shot me a look of disapproval but said nothing. One by one, they all left. The last echoes of engines revving faded into the distance.

I stood in the doorway, motionless through the night, with Samira in my lap. The sun rose. Light poured through the windows.

The front door creaked open.

"Nida?"

Kaushal's voice was gentle, cautious, as if trying to pull me back to reality.

I didn't respond.

He sighed. "Alaul Uncle told me what happened. That you gave Beebo away to the student league dogs. I know you acted in the heat of the moment, but there's still time to fix this. We can bring him back. Send him to a good boarding school. I can make the arrangements and—"

"I never want to hear his name again."

Kaushal exhaled in quiet defeat. Without another word, he lifted Samira from my lap and carried her back inside, talking to her in a soft, cheerful voice, pretending everything was fine.

I remained at the doorway, my body trembling, my mind trapped in shock and disbelief.

Nida | Chapter 7. Protests

Samira had turned five now, and we had a pet cat I named Corporal. I stopped caring about my appearance, letting myself fall into a constant state of disarray. Kaushal urged me to rejoin the workforce, insisting that now that Samira was older, she could stay with a nanny. But I refused—I didn't want to let her out of my sight. I could tell Kaushal disapproved, but he chose not to voice it.

I started tracking his car regularly on my phone, watching him drive to the Watering Hole club once or twice a week. At night, while he slept, I snooped through his phone—his passwords were all just Samira's birthday. His messages to different women weren't romantic, just negotiations—price, time, location. The location was always the Watering Hole. His card transactions showed hotel room charges every time he went there.

It was obvious what he was doing. But he also provided for us, paid for everything I asked for, and was always there for Samira—taking her to school every morning and picking her up during his lunch break. We could afford five chauffeurs, but Kaushal insisted that Samira looked forward to seeing him first after school. And he was right. He also took care of my father and my deranged, lying little brother. He never raised his voice at me. But when I looked at myself in the mirror—dishevelled, losing weight from not eating properly—I realised none of it mattered. Kaushal lost interest in me—either he didn't notice or simply didn't care enough to say anything. And I couldn't bring myself to confront him about what he was doing behind my back.

Alaul started dropping by every weekend in casual clothes to check on us, which was kind of him. He kept me updated on Beebo, though the news was never good. He would chat with me and Samira before heading to the golf course with Kaushal.

Alaul Mofiz, a sixty-something gentleman, had been good friends with Kaushal since my husband took on the role of Chief Overseer, even introducing him to the incredibly dull game of weekend golf. They first met at an income tax collector's daughter's wedding and remained close despite their ongoing debate over the 'right' kind of biryani—because, as Kaushal often said, friendships like theirs brought professional favours, career growth, and influence. It was almost comical how tax officers seemed to cultivate relationships with the country's most prolific figures, while their children flaunted designer goods and overseas vacations on social media. But who would dare question such blatant displays of ill-gotten wealth when the corruption was sanctioned by the taxman himself?

It always seemed like Kaushal treated Alaul as a father figure, and called him "Alaul Uncle" while Alaul often referred to him as "son". Alaul always used his own son as an example, saying that keeping friends who lacked ambition or were drug addicts was pointless. *A symbiotic relationship is necessary—anything else is just parasitic.*

One weekend, I was serving Alaul tea in the living room while he played with Samira, waiting for Kaushal to get ready for golf in the other room.

He spoke, "Nida, it's been over two years. Don't you think Beebo has been punished enough? He's running 'errands' for the government student league that can easily land him in prison for years, if caught red handed. Say the word, and I'll bring him back."

"No," I pushed back.

Alaul sighed. "Nida, I know kids do stupid things. Humayun did idiotic things too. I once had to get him out of a club, high and drunk, completely butt-naked."

Alaul rarely spoke of his son, Humayun—except when using him as a cautionary tale.

I retorted. "This isn't about a wild night gone wrong."

"No, it's usually the choice of company that digs you in deeper," he admitted. "I always told Humayun to stay away from the hoteliers' kids, but he was fixated on impressing *that* girl. She's the one who got him addicted many years ago, and publicly ridiculed me in the process."

I tilted my head. "And what did you do about it?"

"There wasn't much I could do, Nida," he said. "The only thing I managed was... *talking* the tabloid journalist down from publishing more stories."

I shot back, "So you cared more about your public image than your son?"

Alaul didn't flinch. "I did what I had to do to become Chief Inspector. You should be concerned too. Kaushal's *brother-in-law* being kicked out and Beebo joining student league thugs isn't a good look. People only read the headline and make their judgment in five seconds."

I saw what he was saying. With the Turag project in its final stages, Kaushal's reputation needed to be airtight. Most of the mega highways were done, and in five years, Kaushal had achieved more than all the politicians and former Chief Overseers had in thirty—despite taking bribes and working as a lobbyist.

But I stayed firm. "I don't want Beebo coming back into this house."

"It doesn't have to be *this* house," Alaul countered. "You've already kicked him out. We can send him to a school far away. All you need to do is give your consent."

"So that's it? Because I'm his legal guardian?" I scoffed. "I say let him keep paying off his debt to Elias."

Alaul exhaled. "Nida, if this gets out, keeping the press and legal system off your back for *child negligence* will be very hard. They don't care about what you do with Beebo, but they'll go after you just to spite Kaushal."

I narrowed my eyes. "Did Kaushal put you up to this?"

"No," Alaul said firmly. "And I hope you won't tell him we had this conversation."

I let out a humourless chuckle. "Sure. Because all we've been doing lately is keeping secrets. What's one more?"

Kaushal had built an empire and no longer needed my help running it. I got up, took Samira, and walked into her room, shutting the door behind me.

Alaul just watched as our conversation ended abruptly.

...

A few months passed, and news reports began covering student protests erupting across the country. The civilian protesters demanded fairer employment opportunities, ensuring that public office candidates were chosen based on merit rather than fascism or nepotism. However, the official media portrayed a different narrative—unruly student mobs clashing with police officers who were merely struggling to maintain order. Social media, on the other hand, told a much grimmer story. Videos surfaced of police teaming up with political thugs, attacking unarmed students with pistols and machetes. Rickshaws scrambled to carry away lifeless bodies, young children with bullet wounds in their heads, from the conflict zones.

As always, the ruling party chose to meet opposition with brute force. The media reported only what those in power wanted the public to see, while social media became a chaotic battleground of truth and misinformation. Some posts looked so authentic that even I struggled to discern fact from fiction. If I was finding it difficult, I could only imagine how someone like Kaushal's mother was coping. She started her mornings mourning the dead children she saw on social media and ended her nights in tears, praying for her son's safe return from work. She begged him to take a break, to stay home until the situation stabilised, but Kaushal refused. He was adamant about finalising the closing stages of the Turag project, ensuring all the safety tests and certifications were completed.

The highways had been built, but Kaushal kept the entrance and exit junctions offsite, restricting public access until all necessary approvals were secured. To the public, they appeared as massive, unusable roads stretching overhead with no way to get on or off. It was a necessary precaution—early in construction, an inexperienced crane operator had accidentally dropped a concrete slab onto a private car carrying newlyweds. They had sneaked through an unfinished entry junction, hoping to bypass traffic, only to be crushed on impact. The media had a field day, accusing Kaushal of neglecting safety standards without ever questioning why the car was there in the first place.

...

One afternoon, as I sat on the living room sofa braiding Samira's hair, the landline rang. I walked over and picked it up.

"Hello?"

A brief pause, then a voice responded. "Is this Mrs. Nida Oman?"

"Yes."

The voice on the other end continued smoothly, "Ah, a pleasure, Mrs. Nida. This is Sobhanuddin from the Ministry of Road and Transport. I trust you remember me?"

Ignoring his question, I replied flatly, "Kaushal isn't home."

"Yes, I'm aware," he said, his tone shifting slightly. "We had a bit of a disagreement, and he stopped answering my calls. Now tell me, is that any way to treat a long-time supporter?"

I kept my voice neutral. "I don't know what you two spoke about. He doesn't share much with me these days. I can't help you."

His voice hardened. "You weren't so distant when accepting 'gifts,' Mrs. Nida."

"I can pay you back for all of it," I snapped.

A low chuckle. "Your husband offered the same. It's not about money—it's about goodwill, Mrs. Nida."

I exhaled, irritated. "Why are you calling our home?"

"I wouldn't have to if Kaushal just listened to instructions," he said. Then, lowering his voice, "Mrs. Nida, would you mind if I called you on WhatsApp? This isn't the kind of conversation best had over a landline."

Something in his tone made me hesitate, but for reasons I couldn't quite explain, I agreed and gave him my number. A moment later, my phone buzzed with his call.

When I answered, he spoke bluntly. "This is a terrible time to complete the Turag project, as you well know. We at the ministry have repeatedly advised Kaushal to postpone the launch by a year—long enough for the ruling party to clean up this student protest mess. Then, we'd host a grand unveiling of the highways to help the public forget all about it. But your husband refuses to listen."

I quickly argued. "Kaushal takes his work very seriously."

"He also takes bribery seriously," Sobhanuddin countered. "We asked him to name his price, but he wouldn't. Said he had more to lose if he backed down—claimed he'd already made international press announcements on behalf of Sigmoid promising completion in a few months."

I sighed. "Well, he doesn't work for the government, Sobhanuddin."

He sighed, "We even got the board at Sigmoid to try talking him down, but he still wouldn't budge. Said he values his reputation and the promises he's made... What an altruistic hypocrite."

Frustration bubbled inside me. "If he's being such a problem for you, why not just get Sigmoid to fire him?"

A dry chuckle. "Fire someone for doing their job well? The state is already drowning in bad social media press for attacking students. Firing the man responsible for making the Turag project a reality would create the perfect storm."

I frowned. "Then why are you calling me?"

"Mrs. Nida," he said, his voice lowering to something almost persuasive, "talk to your husband. Tell him to take a step back. Go on a vacation—maybe a safari trip overseas—while we handle things here. I don't want things to be difficult for you and your daughter here amidst the public unrest."

The last bit sounded almost like a threat. I tightened my grip on the phone, refusing to respond to his threats. "I appreciate your call, Sobhanuddin, but please don't ever call here again."

And I hung up.

That night, I waited in front of the door for Kaushal to return from work to tell him about Sobhanuddin's call. When he finally came home, he was completely disinterested, brushing off my concerns no matter how much I emphasised the urgency of the situation. I followed him from the entryway to the bathroom, where he washed his face, then to the closet as he changed. But every time I tried to bring it up, he shut me down.

"I know what the man wants from me," he said, his voice flat. "And I won't entertain his absurd requests at the expense of *my*...", He paused, searching for the right word before finally saying, "...reputation."

I scoffed. "What reputation, Kaushal? The only reason you even took up this role was because I pushed you to do it. You said so yourself. You listened to me then, why not now?"

He exhaled sharply, turning to face me. But when he spoke, his voice was calm as always. "Nida, I never wanted this position. My goal was to expose the fraud, not lead it."

"And end up six feet under," I shot back. "I saved you from yourself."

He gave a small, bitter chuckle. "And dug me into a deeper mess with the missing gold necklace. Because of that, I had to start laundering money. That was the mess you got us into."

I never told him that I had seen proof at the principal's office that Beebo had, in fact, stolen the necklace. But in the heat of that moment,

I felt the need to defend myself from what felt like an accusation, to remind him of my role in his success.

I smirked in sarcasm. "And look at you now—an entire business empire under your belt. All thanks to me."

He tensed but kept his composure. "Nida, yes, you wrote my speeches and taught me how to present myself. But after that, you left me to 'do whatever I thought was best.' You merely suggested that we had to do something about the bribe money without giving me any direction."

I snapped, frustration mounting at how calmly he was speaking. "Well, because I've never laundered money before!"

His expression remained unreadable. "You say that like I've been taking bribes and laundering money all my life. I just tried to make the best of the situation—to get paid fairly for my work, just like you taught me."

He was admitting my role in all of this yet somehow, I still felt like I was losing. I refused to lose this argument, so I pivoted. "Forget the bribery. It's simply not safe to leave home nowadays. Is your reputation really more important than your own safety? Think about your mother—how she worries every time you walk out that door."

For the first time, Kaushal hesitated. "It's not that simple, Nida. I can't just up and put the entire project on hold."

"Why not?"

His voice grew distant, almost weary. "Because I just want to finish the Turag Project and be done with everything tied to it. Nida, this project has been a disaster from the start. Government records claimed that people had sold their land for highway construction, but many never actually received payment. Whether they were telling the truth or if this was just another case of property fraud didn't matter—I was told by the board to 'convince' them by any means necessary.

The logistics had been a mess for thirty years. Fake receipts were submitted for purchases, but no inventory ever existed. Contractors listed on official documents reported transactions that never occurred with the tax office—classic tax fraud. When I confronted them with the evidence, they denied everything outright, and the board warned me to stay within my limits. So I had to start from scratch, brokering new deals that respected the five year deadline that tore every ethical fibre in my being—far worse than any petty lobbying bribes."

Kaushal walked out of the room and peeked into Samira's, watching for a moment as she slept peacefully. Letting out a quiet sigh, he returned to the bedroom, his voice lower but still firm as he continued, "then we discovered a mass grave—probably a dumping ground from the rebellions in the nineties. The families of the deceased refused to let us build over it, calling the land sacred, even though they'd been dumping trash on it for decades. We had to change the entire plan midway to accommodate their sentiments. And all this time, I was being pressured—lobbied, threatened, urged to hand out jobs to relatives of powerful people. I never told you because I didn't want to worry you.

For the past five years, the seniors I bypassed on my way to the top have been waiting for me to fail. When that didn't happen, they resorted to anonymous corruption allegations against me. They've already fed journalists sensitive internal information that could be used to incriminate me, convinced that I'll never see this project through. I had to ask Alaul Uncle to ensure those reports never made it to the public and that the journalists were kept silent so I could keep pushing forward. But if I back down now, I'll be proving them right.

But we're so close, Nida. The student protests won't affect construction—it's already done. We're just waiting for compliance approvals from overseas assessors. Once we get the green light, we place the junctions and toll booths, and that's it."

I looked at him and said quietly, "Kaushal, what happens if Sobhanuddin sends people like Elias to come after Samira? Does your reputation matter more than her safety?"

I chose not to mention that I had been tracking his car to the Watering Hole—it wasn't relevant to this conversation.

Kaushal's stubbornness didn't waver. "Enough, Nida. You talk like I'm the one putting Samira in danger, when it was Beebo who invited Elias into our home. God knows how many other things he's done that put you and Samira at risk.

So please, let me handle this. Two more months, and we're done. No grand unveiling like Sobhanuddin wants—no ceremony to let the government take credit for work they didn't do. I'll just open the roads and walk away. Then I'll quit Sigmoid, cash out from the businesses. We'll take the money we've already made and leave. Far away from here."

If only I could believe it would be that simple.

...

A week later, social media exploded with videos of political goons from the student league firing pistol rounds at unarmed students—young protesters armed with nothing but water bottles and grocery bags, distributing food among their peers. In one of the videos, a familiar figure stood out. Beebo. He was gripping a pistol, firing relentlessly at children. My stomach twisted as I watched in horror. Assisting him were several men in police uniforms, their shotguns aimed in the same direction as his pistol. My jaw dropped, and before I knew it, tears streamed down my face.

Samira noticed my distress and walked up to me with Corporal in her arms. "Ma, what happened?"

I struggled to find words—how could I explain such brutality to a child? Instead, I took the coward's way out. "I just remembered my father, your grandfather... and felt sad."

She wrapped her tiny arms around me, patting my back with the purest of reassurances. "Don't worry, Ma. I'm here for you."

Within hours, social media detectives flooded online pages with photos and identities of every student league thug involved in the shooting. The name that stood out most prominently: *Bashir Oman*—Beebo. The comment sections seethed with rage, filled with threats from furious citizens and keyboard warriors declaring what they would do if they ever found him. As much as I knew Beebo deserved whatever was coming, I couldn't shake the sinking guilt that I had failed him—not just as a sister, but as a guardian.

Unsure of what to do, I picked up the phone and called Alaul. My voice came out in a whisper. "You have my consent. Please send Beebo far away. Please."

On the other end, I could hear a bit of the chaos—tear gas canisters popping, the frantic shouting of police officers ordering the angry mob to stand down. Alaul remained silent for a moment, likely issuing orders. Then he finally responded with a voice devoid of its usual confidence.

"I'm sorry, Nida. It's beyond that point now. No matter how this conflict plays out, Beebo cannot be saved. So are the policemen who stood with him."

...

By August 5, the nation had reached its breaking point. Students, parents, and children from every corner of the country marched to the capital. The military, taking a neutral stance, did not interfere as the protests swelled into a full-scale uprising. Faced with overwhelming resistance, the police forces stepped down. And then, in an unprecedented turn, the ruling party—after years of unopposed dictatorship and election fraud—resigned from office.

Chaos followed.

Many key political figures, including Sobhanuddin and the Sigmoid board members, vanished—some slipping into hiding, others fleeing the country with forged passports. The lesser politicians and police officers, lacking the same resources, attempted to escape into rural villages. But there, they met a different fate—angry villagers captured them, tied them to trees, and left them to starve. Some died before the military arrived days later to retrieve their broken bodies.

In the midst of it all, Kaushal didn't need to halt the Turag Project. In the end, everything worked out for him.

Or so I thought.

But when you leave a country in the hands of a politically unversed public, lawlessness takes root. First, it was common thugs seizing the opportunity to loot small businesses. Then came the opposition parties, quick to stake their claim, setting fire to every enterprise linked to the now-fallen regime—jobs be damned. And then there were the clueless mobs, storming former political leaders' homes, parading around in their stolen undergarments, celebrating with a tasteless display of victory.

When the dust settled, some regions elected influential figures with extreme religious viewpoints, who began putting forward plans to end secularism. As controversial as their views were, they were the only ones providing for the impoverished locals. A starving man will elect anyone who puts food in his belly, regardless of their beliefs.

That was when *the video* started circulating.

It came from multiple angles, filmed by countless members of the crowd. The footage showed a raging mob stringing up a man by the ankle, suspending him upside down—just like livestock prepared for slaughter. The man's hands were bound, and a large brown bag was secured tightly around his head, tied at the neck with a rope. With each desperate gasp, the bag inflated and deflated as the man struggled for air. The man was frail, almost skeletal, like he hadn't eaten for days. The crowd beat him mercilessly with sticks and bats like a piñata, striking until his body ceased all movement. But they weren't finished. They plunged knives into his corpse, spitting on it, kicking it—turning it into something grotesquely unrecognisable.

One version of the video included a voiceover from the uploader with their tone laced with sadistic amusement.

"Folks, we got one of the student league dogs from the shooting videos. The people served justice today. Ladies and gentlemen, presenting the now *expired* Bashir Oman!"

Nida | Chapter 8. Happily never after

I sat on the sofa, crying my eyes out as Kaushal kept calling my phone. It buzzed repeatedly until it finally fell silent. Moments later, Kaushal's mother walked out of her room, pressing her phone to her ear as she spoke, "Yes, poor thing is crying her eyes out. She won't even let me near her."

She wasn't wrong. She had woken up from her afternoon nap to the sound of my wailing and, in her usual kindness, offered her company. But I didn't want to be comforted—I just wanted to be left alone.

"Kaushal wants to talk to you, sweetie," she said, holding the phone out to me. I shook my head. She took the hint and quietly retreated to her room.

An hour later, Kaushal arrived to find me in the exact same spot, unmoved from the sofa. He knelt down to hug me, but I pushed him away.

His voice was gentle. "Alaul Uncle told me. I'm sorry, Nida. I asked him to recover whatever is left of Beebo so we can give him a proper burial."— Sadly, that never happened. By the time the mob was done with him, he was indistinguishable from the other thugs they had flayed alive.

I acknowledged his words with a nod, still weeping. He sat beside me, silent, waiting. Eventually, I spoke. "Please leave me alone. I'll call you if I need something."

This wasn't about pushing him away—it was about not wanting him to waste his time on me. The Turag Project's completion and opening were due in two weeks, and I knew he was already overwhelmed.

He hesitated, insisting a few times before finally relenting. "Call me if you need anything."

After Kaushal left, I turned on the news. The media had already shifted their narrative, now condemning the crimes of the fallen government. People switched sides so easily to protect their own interests.

My social media flooded with hate messages from strangers—people I had never met—calling me every name imaginable, linking me to everything Beebo had done, and threatening unspeakable things. Social media detectives and keyboard warriors had done their usual work, digging up family ties and targeting everyone connected, as if bad deeds were somehow inherited in this country. They likely chose this moment to strike, assuming Kaushal was politically tied to the fallen regime, believing we had no political influence to retaliate against the hate. That assumption was partially correct; we had no authority to fight back—but that was because we were not directly affiliated with any political party. The hatred seemed to stem less from me being related to Beebo and more from the fact that Kaushal never publicly supported the student rebellion.

Student protesters felt entitled to the support of all known media figures, believing they had to show solidarity. In reality, Kaushal was so engrossed in the Turag Project throughout the year that he didn't even have time to doomscroll through social media, let alone engage with the constant stream of demoralising content. He had enough negativity in his life already. He also didn't have a public relations manager handling his social media feed to send out messages that were neither authentic, nor genuine.

Within the hour, I received over a hundred hate messages, forcing me to deactivate all my accounts just to find some peace.

I felt colder than usual—whether from fear, grief for Beebo, or simply the fact that I hadn't eaten all day, I couldn't tell. I pulled on a warm sweater, hoping it would help stave off the chill. But deep down, I knew this cold wasn't going anywhere anytime soon.

Thankfully, Samira never had to go hungry. Kaushal's mother made sure she was fed, never asking me anymore after too many refusals. She focused on Samira, which was all I ever wanted.

...

One week went by.

Kaushal returned home early one evening and sat beside me on the sofa as I stared at the turned-off TV. He noticed my sleeveless turtleneck sweater dress and casually untied his own tie, as if to show how hot it was outside.

He joked, "How are you not sweating in that? It's so warm out there!"

I heard him, but chose not to respond.

I was lost in my thoughts. If I didn't know better, I would have sworn I was hearing all the hate messages personified into voices in my head—it felt so vivid.

"Where's Samira?" he asked, hoping to engage me.

"Playing with your mother," I answered flatly. "You're back early."

He sighed. "Yeah. The board of directors at Sigmoid changed. Most of them are long-time supporters of the opposition party now..."

"So?" I interrupted, not getting the point. Then I caught myself and apologised. "I'm sorry, I got carried away again. Please continue."

Kaushal nodded. "The new board called me in today. They want me to pause the project until the opposition formally takes control of the country next year."

I frowned. "Why? What do they gain from that?"

"They plan to leverage the Turag Project to take another loan from the World Bank, claiming the protests damaged it beyond repair."

"Was it damaged?"

"No," Kaushal said firmly. "Not at all. Which means that entire loan will go straight into the pockets of key opposition party members once they take office. These party members will lobby in favour of Sigmoid. Then Sigmoid will secure its place as the government's preferred contractor for most future projects."

Nothing changed. The faces in power shifted, but the corruption remained. Nobody wanted the Turag Project completed—it had always been a massive scam.

I looked at Kaushal, knowing how blunt he could be. "What did you say to them?"

Kaushal smiled. "I told them I quit. I refuse to be a part of this any longer."

I was baffled. "Just like that?"

Kaushal nodded. "There was no winning here, Nida. I tried for five years. I think that's long enough to know if something's going to work out or not."

I asked, "How did the board take it?"

Kaushal mocked their voices. "You can't resign. The media will want explanations."

I followed up, "And?"

Kaushal continued, "I told them that if that's what they want, I'll release a media statement detailing all the work we've done and explain that I'm resigning to spend more time with my family."

His response seemed reasonable. "And what did they say?"

"They said my name is now synonymous with the Turag Project. The only way they can secure the loan is if I'm the one to submit the request to the World Bank... in other words, they want me at the forefront of international fraud."

I sighed. "So what happened then?"

Kaushal exhaled with a smile of relief. "I resigned. Tomorrow will be my last official day at work. The day after, I'll hold a press conference handing over the project to whoever they choose as my replacement."

I hesitated. "Kaushal... won't your resignation affect the company's public image? What are you planning to say in the press release?"

He reached for my hand, squeezing it gently. "Whatever you write for me."

That bit of reassurance—his trust in me—made me smile for the first time in days. He pulled me close, and I buried my face in his chest, letting the tears come.

That night, as we sat on our bed drafting the media statement, Kaushal asked, "So, where do you and Samira want to move to?"

I blinked. "Move?"

He nodded. "After I resign, we're free to go wherever we want. We have the means to start fresh. Pick a place, and we'll move there for good. Just one condition—my mom is coming with us."

I laughed. "Kaushal, Samira enjoys your mother's company."

Kaushal squinted playfully as he realised that I chose to mention Samira instead of myself, and we both burst into laughter.

For the first time in years, he wasn't burdened by the project. We spent hours browsing cities and schools for Samira, imagining a completely new life.

Then his phone rang. It was Alaul. Kaushal put it on speaker, wanting me to hear everything from now on.

"I'm sorry, Kaushal," Alaul said.

Kaushal frowned. "What happened, Uncle?"

"Tune in to the news. It's airing now."

We ran to the living room, switching on the television. Every channel was broadcasting the same breaking news:

"Surveillance footage exposes Turag Project Chief Overseer, Kaushal Veni, at the Watering Hole with actress Pixie Chandan. The footage captures him getting her drunk, taking her to a hotel room, and proceeding to sexually assault her. Pixie says mental trauma kept her silent all this time but is now going to pursue legal action against Kaushal Veni."

Kaushal questioned himself in shock, "She was an actress? "

Kaushal turned to me, panic in his eyes. "Nida, what they're saying is not true. Yes, I went to the Watering Hole several times, but I never forced myself on anyone."

I kept my voice even. "I knew about the Watering Hole. I tracked your car's GPS."

He looked stunned. "You're not angry?"

I sighed. "Kaushal, I know you've paid for sex before. I'm not happy about it, but I also know I haven't been perfect either. You've had to put up with a lot because of Beebo too."

He stared at me in disbelief. "I was almost certain you'd come at me with a knife or something."

I smirked looking down at the turtleneck I was wearing in the middle of summer. "I do look like one of those crazy cat ladies with messy hair and weird outfits, don't I?" I then looked up and spoke firmly, "But seriously, I want you to stop hiring escorts. Period."

Kaushal exhaled in relief. "Of course. I promise."

I pivoted to the pressing concern. "Now tell me how you got involved with an aspiring B-grade actress like Pixie Chandan."

Kaushal looked visibly shaken. "Nida, she never told me her real name—I had no idea she was an actress."

I asked, "Was this part of the accusations your colleagues anonymously put forward to the press that Alaul had to cover up?"

Kaushal replied, "No. I never told Alaul Uncle about what I do at the Watering Hole."

I picked up where he left off. "Then I have a feeling she was planted as a failsafe by Sigmod, and now this was leaked to discredit you—so the board can claim they fired you instead of you resigning. Preserving their public image is more important, especially since they have no idea what you plan to disclose in your media statement."

An hour later, A Sigmoid Human Resources representative called Kaushal, seemingly unaware that he had already handed in his resignation. They informed him that he was officially fired, effective immediately, and that the press conference had been cancelled.

Kaushal was tensing up. I placed a reassuring hand on his arm. "Don't worry, Kaushal. We got what we wanted, and they got their

Turag Scam back. Now, we just have to pay Pixie Chandan whatever she's trying to extort from us with this bogus lawsuit, and we can walk away."

He nodded, though I could tell he wasn't entirely convinced. Before we could process the situation, a loud knock echoed at our front door. When we opened the door, we found Alaul standing there, flanked by several police officers. His expression was apologetic as he said, "Look, Kaushal, I'm sorry, but we just received a warrant to urgently search your property. I wanted to come down personally to make sure the men don't damage anything. Please cooperate so we can get this over with."

Kaushal stiffened but stepped aside, allowing them in. Alaul turned to the officers and instructed, "Be careful. Don't take or damage anything unnecessarily."

As they moved through our home, methodically searching every corner—including the empty safe in the closet—Alaul motioned for us to sit in the living room. He then leaned in, speaking to Kaushal in a hushed tone. I could barely hear, so I shifted closer just in time to catch his words.

"You stepping down right after the ruling party did raised concerns for the interim government, which is now dominated by the opposition. You're being investigated for all the bribes you allegedly took during the last five years of the Turag Project."

I scoffed. "And what exactly is this search supposed to prove? Did they really think Kaushal would just leave piles of bribe money lying around?"

Knowing him, he might have in brown bags all over the house if it weren't for me—but that was beside the point.

Alaul sighed. "This isn't really about finding anything. It's a scare tactic. They want to make sure you don't speak to the public."

It was painfully clear. There had always been a choice—refuse the first bribe. But after taking it, the only options left were to keep going or face the consequences for the ones you had already accepted.

Alaul continued, "If they don't find an obscene amount of cash here, we'll instruct the banks to unfreeze your accounts."

Kaushal's face darkened. "Our bank accounts are frozen?"

Alaul nodded. "Yes. At the same time we received the warrant"

The search turned up nothing, as expected. But the damage had already been done—watching officers rifle through her personal belongings left Kaushal's elderly mother visibly shaken.

As the officers filed out, Alaul lingered at the door. He looked at us for a moment, then simply said, "I'm sorry," before walking away.

As Alaul left, I turned to Kaushal. "We have something outside the banks, right?"

Kaushal stayed silent, as if piecing things together in his head. After a moment, he finally spoke. "The investment accounts are all linked to my bank account... and by association, to yours." He trailed off, mumbling something under his breath that I couldn't make out before circling back with a resigned, "No. All the money in the accounts was clean—I never felt the need to move cash aside."

"Then we wait until this clears up... whenever that is."

But we never got the chance to wait it out.

The news reported that Pixie was discussing the details of the "tragic" event on social media. Kaushal took his phone and opened his social media profile in front of me, revealing thousands of unread messages, most likely hate messages similar to the ones I received from people we didn't know.

Pixie took to social media, crying and sulking about all the 'terrible' things Kaushal had supposedly done to her—conveniently leaving out the part where she was paid to be his escort. Renowned media personalities backed her up, showering her with sympathy, and her follower count skyrocketed. Any publicity is good publicity it seemed.

Then the threats started.

Strangers—people Kaushal had never even met—sent him death threats over phone, and soon enough, I started receiving them too. Somehow, they got a hold of our phone numbers. Our phones rang all night, one threat after another, until we had no choice but to switch them off.

Then, late that night, a sound of shattering glass echoed through our home followed by a heavy thud.

We rushed out to find that someone had thrown a brick through Samira's window.

We rushed to the shattered window just in time to hear a motorcycle speeding away, the rider screaming, "That's what you get for what you did to Pixie!"

Samira was shaking, tears streaming down her face as I held her, trying to comfort her. Meanwhile, Kaushal grabbed some cardboard and duct tape, sealing up the broken window and cutting the edges clean with a box cutter.

This was getting out of hand.

Kaushal switched his phone back on. "Let me try to fix this," he said, dialling every influential contact he knew in the media.

No one picked up.

By the second round of calls, some numbers went straight to voicemail, while others started beeping—blocked. We were completely alone in this. One day, Kaushal was a respected public figure. The next, he had become the internet's most hated man.

Just before dawn, Alaul returned with tired eyes and a group of officers. He likely hadn't even had the chance to go home from his office, as I could tell by the small black bag he was carrying under his arm with casual clothes spilling out from top.

His expression was grim as he handed over an official order: Kaushal was to be placed under house arrest until his trial against Pixie—three months from now. Until then, all his *and* our joint bank accounts would remain frozen, with only a minimal allowance for basic living expenses, effectively cutting off his access to legal representation and any chance of survival beyond the bare minimum.

It was remarkable how swiftly or slowly the justice system moved when it served those in power.

I folded my arms and stared at Alaul. "If the accounts stay frozen, how the hell are we supposed to hire a lawyer?"

Alaul hesitated, fidgeting with the sling of the small black slouch bag he had brought with him before signalling for his men to wait outside. Once they left, he turned to Kaushal. "I've already been warned by the magistrate not to involve myself in a case beneath the Chief Inspector, so I imagine this will be the last time I can personally intervene. I need to make this quick." He paused, then looked at me. "Can I get some tea, Nida?"

I narrowed my eyes. "I'm not going anywhere."

"Nida, please," he sighed. "I have to leave soon, but I need to speak with Kaushal alone."

Kaushal placed a reassuring hand on my arm. "It's okay, Nida. I'll fill you in later, I promise."

Reluctantly, I stepped away, not to grab tea, but straight into Samira's room. My mind raced with possibilities as I tried to silence the voices rambling in my head, each jumping to a new conclusion. What were they talking about? What was Alaul hiding?

I turned on the surveillance feed and cranked up the volume on the living room camera, but it was clear Kaushal anticipated that move. He and Alaul both turned away from the camera and began whispering, with Alaul gesturing toward the black bag at one point. I realised this was pointless, so I turned off the feed and sat there with Samira, gently petting Corporal.

Half an hour later, Kaushal walked in, his face pale, his eyes red-rimmed. The first thing he did was ask Samira to take Corporal and go play with his mother in the other room. Once Samira was out, He looked at me, his voice shaky. "Nida... I just need you to play along, okay?"

I frowned. "Play along with what, Kaushal?"

He didn't answer immediately. A single tear slid down his cheek before he inhaled deeply, forcing himself to regain composure.

He stepped closer as I remained seated on Samira's bed. "Kaushal, you're scaring me. Please, just tell me what's going on."

He kneeled to my level, speaking slowly and softly. "They're placing me under indefinite house arrest. Because I know too much."

I stiffened. "What do you mean?"

"I know all of the dirty secrets surrounding the Turag Project."

I swallowed hard. "Kaushal... they don't put 'loose ends' under house arrest indefinitely, they get rid—" I froze mid-sentence as realisation dawned on me. My breath hitched. "Kaushal, what is this actually about?"

He forced a weak smile. "My mom will take Samira to her sister's place for a few days. And Alaul Uncle... he's going to arrest you."

I blinked. "Arrest me? For what?"

Kaushal met my gaze. "For stabbing me in self-defence."

The room suddenly felt suffocating. "Defending myself from what?"

His voice was steady now. "From the same monster that attacked Pixie Chandan. The media will know that you exposed me for my corruption after tolerating physical abuse for years."

I pushed back. "Kaushal... you're out of your mind."

"No, I already spoke to Alaul Uncle," he continued. "You'll be taken into custody and testify that you fought back and stabbed me when I forced myself onto you. Uncle will help you press charges against me, that you wanted to leave me, but I kept you by force... and if I don't fight the allegations..."

I recoiled. "What?! Kaushal, no—"

His eyes softened. "Once you're bailed out, Alaul Uncle will help you get access to our joint account. It's where most of our money is, anyway. The government will seize everything solely in my name including all our businesses, whether it's clean or not. This is the only way to make sure you and Samira have something left."

Tears blurred my vision. "Kaushal, what are you asking me to do?"

"Don't worry, love," he said gently, brushing his thumb over my cheek. "Alaul Uncle promised that he will be there to guide you. He'll make sure the media doesn't publish anything until you're bailed out. Otherwise, an angry mob might storm the station with half-baked information, making it harder to manage the media narrative. Just stick to the story until they let you out and unfreeze the account."

My hands trembled. "Convincing... how? My mind isn't even working right now."

Kaushal scanned the room, his gaze landing on the box cutter he had mistakenly left in the corner. Before I could react, he grabbed it, clicked it open, and shoved it into my hand. Then, in one swift motion, he pressed himself onto the blunt blade, barely nicking his skin. Dramatically, he gasped, "Ow! You stabbed me!"

His performance was terrible. He even winked at me afterward with his teary eyes.

Right on cue, Alaul stepped inside, his face expressionless. He pulled out a plastic evidence bag and a pair of gloves. "Mrs. Nida Oman, you are under arrest for attacking Kaushal Veni." He met my eyes. "Come, now let's get you out of here."

Kaushal said nothing. He simply stood there, silent tears rolling down his cheeks.

Alaul turned to Kaushal's mother who was staring on from the other room. "Ma'am, please take Samira and the cat and leave with me."

She panicked. "Kaushal—he's not coming?"

Kaushal managed a smile. "It'll be okay, Mom. Just look after Samira and Corporal until Nida is out."

As I turned to leave, Alaul paused. "Would you like to change out of that turtleneck? It's warm outside."

I shook my head. I couldn't care less.

The last thing Kaushal said before I was taken away was the one thing that keeps playing in my head even now.

"If you get bailed out in 48 hours, please do not log into the surveillance feed."

As we walked out, I noticed that the black slouch bag Alaul had carried in was no longer with him.

Yaad | Epilogue

I watched as Nida sat there in front of me, tears rolling down her cheeks as she gripped the jail door bars for support. I placed my hand over hers on the cold metal and said softly, "I'm sorry, I had no idea."

Nida shook her head as she spoke. "It's okay. I've almost come to terms with it all. I just needed someone to come and get me out."

I replied, "I should have taken Alaul's messages more seriously. I had no idea he was the Chief Inspector and so involved in your story. I'm sorry for leaving you alone in this."

Nida responded, "We often forget how alone we are until something like this happens—until you realise that no one will be there for you when you need them."

"I'm sorry I didn't arrive on time."

The sound of heavy boots echoed through the corridor. Morning had already broken, and through the door walked a tall, well-built man, likely in his sixties with short, grey curly hair and a neatly trimmed grey beard. The officer at the desk immediately stood up and saluted. "Good morning, Chief Inspector. The brother is here."

The man's sharp gaze locked onto me as I sat on the floor holding Nida's hand. His expression unreadable, he replied, "Yes, I can see that."

As he walked past Hafiz's cell, Hafiz suddenly sprang to his feet. "Mofiz sir! Am I glad to see you! That's a nice cologne, the fragrance really suits you!" He continued, attempting to flatter the Chief Inspector, "You know, sir, I've always said how corrupt the ex-regime was. I'm so relieved that you're still in charge and not one of them because—"

Alaul shot him a withering glare that shut him up instantly. His voice was cold as he said, "You wouldn't happen to be the one the men mentioned was screaming 'double standards' when we arrested you, would you? People like you switch political sides faster than they switch soiled underwear."

Hafiz, shocked and embarrassed by what the Chief Inspector said, retreated to the corner of his cell as Alaul resumed walking toward me.

I stood up as he approached and extended his hand. With a firm grip, he shook my hand and said, "Chief Inspector of Dhaka Division, Alaul Mofiz. Thank you for finally showing up, Dr. Oman."

I met his gaze and replied, "Nida has brought me up to speed."

He glanced at Nida uneasily and sighed. "Of course. I'd like to get this over with. Follow me."

Nida motioned for me to follow him. As we walked past the front desk, I noticed another officer had just taken over the shift at the front desk and was now speaking with Hafiz's wife.

Alaul rolled his eyes as we passed them. He led me to the largest office in the back, a room reserved for the head of the station. "We'll borrow this room until my colleague shows up from hiding or is replaced. It'll give us time to talk privately."

I followed him in as he took a seat and gestured for me to sit across from him.

I sat, and he spoke, "You took your time, Dr. Oman."

I responded, "It's hard to take anyone on WhatsApp seriously. Especially when you introduce yourself as a simple officer rather than *the* Chief of Police!"

Alaul nodded. "I imagine Nida has already told you everything, so I'll ask for your understanding regarding my discretion. My involvement in the Kaushal Veni case is already toeing the line of an internal investigation—I'd rather not make it worse. Besides, would you have believed me if I had messaged you saying, 'This is the Dhaka Chief of Police'?"

I considered his point, and it made sense. "That would have probably convinced me immediately that it was a scam."

Then, pressing the conversation forward, I asked, "Is Kaushal okay?"

He looked at me with a faint sigh. "You didn't see the news?" He opened his phone, scrolled through and opened something up and handed it to me. Several headlines from yesterday evening flashed across the brightly lit screen with enlarged fonts:

"The Curse of the Turag Project Claims Another Chief Overseer!"

"Turag Project Overseer Kaushal Veni Shoots Himself, Fearing Prosecution"

"The Animal Kaushal Veni Attacks Helpless Wife After She Exposes His Corruption"

"Actress Pixie Chandan Dances in Celebration of the Death of the Man Who Sexually Assaulted Her, Congratulates Wife for Representing Courage and Becoming a Role Model for All Women"

I had read enough and handed the phone back to him. "Tell me honestly, when and how did he actually die?"

Alaul paused before replying, "Gunshot wound: entry through the roof of the mouth, exit through the back of the head. He took his own life the day after Nida allegedly stabbed him. We deliberately withheld the news from the media until we could conduct a *proper* investigation."

He was only being partially honest. Based on how Nida had described Alaul to me, he likely tried to keep the media quiet for as long as he could until he could get Nida out of the picture. Maybe he was already struggling to control the press, which was why he felt the need to persistently message me until I confirmed that I was on my way.

I replied, "Kaushal was never the type of person to carry a gun. And how did that not show up when you raided the house under warrant?"

He hesitated, once again holding back the full truth. "Officially, I'll say he probably hid it very well."

I challenged him, "That would mean the police didn't do their job very well. It wouldn't happen to have been hidden in a black slouch bag, would it?"

He ignored my deliberate provocation. "Look, Dr. Oman... *Yaad*, Kaushal was more like a son to me than a friend. While I can't speak to how he got a gun or comment on his actions, I'll tell you this—the alternative would have been much worse. Him taking control of his life at the end and leaving a confession letter clearing Nida of everything made the case much easier to close on our end. As it stands now, all charges against Nida have been dropped, and their joint accounts are now unfrozen."

He stopped, almost contemplating how to say the next part in a politically correct way, before deciding to just go with whatever was on his mind. "Had things gone differently, we likely would have had a homicide on our hands, and it would have taken as long as the Turag Project to solve, with all his money withheld from his family as evidence until the case was closed."

He looked around at the corners and walls, almost as if checking for surveillance cameras before speaking again. "Off the record, there is some truth to the 'curse' surrounding the Turag Project. Some of the previous Chief Overseers were murdered, and the cases are still under investigation to this day. None of the surviving Ex-Overseers want to speak out, likely terrified they'll meet the same fate. But Kaushal's sacrifice ensured Nida is free to raise Samira, just as he would have wanted."

The problem was, Nida could never go back to being the person she was after everything that happened. She told me Hafiz had been whispering his innocence for the last two days, yet Hafiz, his wife, and the desk officer confirmed that he was only brought in last afternoon. And Nida, who's quite deaf, should *not* have been able to pick up what Hafiz was mumbling in the cell so far away unless he started screaming, like he did when I arrived. She kept telling me, as she brought me up to speed, that she had been hearing voices for a while.

I nodded as there was no point in discussing it with Alaul. The priority was getting Nida out first. That was where the topic of bail money came in.

I spoke up, "About the bail money, I was mugged yesterday on my way to the station and lost both the bail money and my passport."

Alaul sighed, "Your family has had a rough run of luck, Yaad. I tried to get the judge to waive the bail fees in the first place. Hold on, let me follow up and see what I can do for you."

He stepped out of the room to make a call. A few minutes later, he returned with good news. "The judge who set the bail order is a friend. He's agreed to waive the fees. Honestly, it was a bit easier to convince him once I pointed out that the bail was based on Kaushal being a flight risk. Now that the media knows he's gone and the confession letter is out, it was much easier. You will have to naturally claim responsibility for Nida. But she's is free to go, Yaad."

I looked at Alaul in disbelief, "Just like that?"

He replied, "Consider this my final favour for a dearly departed friend. I tried doing for him exactly what I would have probably done for my own son, if he had ever ended up in Kaushal's shoes."

I quickly followed up on that, "How is Humayun?"

Alaul smiled, "You know Humayun?"

I nodded, "I did, from a while back. And Nida told me he was your son."

I remembered what I read in Sufi's diary about what happened to Humayun at Amjad's party that night.

Alaul's smile faded into a sombre expression as he said, "Then you should come see him at our home sometime. I can't guarantee he'll recognise you—drugs have eaten away at his cognitive functions—but it would be nice for him to have a visitor after all these years."

"I'll try, but no promises," I replied.

Alaul nodded. "Of course, you have your own things to worry about."

I couldn't help but wonder what had happened to Elias, given how much of a problem he seemed to be in Nida's story.

"So, Nida mentioned a student politics leader..."

Alaul cut in immediately. "You mean Elias? I always found it amusing how a forty-year-old man with no formal education managed to run in student politics—just because he knew how to intimidate educated students."

I pressed further. "So what exactly happened to him once the government fell and Beebo... well, you know."

Alaul's voice carried a note of sympathy. "What happened to Beebo was unfortunate and easily preventable. He could have had a good life if he hadn't chased money and fame, and if Nida had just stopped being so stubborn about so many things."

Then, as if recalling something funny, he smirked. "The moment the government collapsed, Elias scraped together all his savings and paid a migration dealer to smuggle him into America in a shipping container through Africa and South America."

I was curious. "And that's funny because?"

Alaul chuckled. "Because he walked straight into a migration scam. We cracked down on the dealer the next day and the man was quick to snitch on him. We knew exactly what Elias was up to and let him do it. The American border authorities are already aware of his route. He's going to get caught after he arrives at the American border in six months and deported back to Bangladesh."

I smirked. "Sounds like he got what he deserved."

Alaul sighed. "If only his friends and family felt the same way. Instead, I know they'll spin a sob story about how Elias was denied a better life in America—claiming how he had big dreams but no choice but to migrate via an illegal path because he couldn't speak basic English."

I picked up where he left off. "So they'll run their own sympathy scam. But who's actually going to buy it?"

Alaul laughed. "Elias will likely pin his hopes on the Western media—just as the goons before him did—spinning a sob story in the hopes that a European country will grant him asylum on humanitarian grounds. Little does he know that the Western world has grown wiser to these scams, and he's in for big trouble."

I frowned. "Why would he be in trouble?"

"Once he gets sent back to Bangladesh and the public recognises him on the streets, they will tear him apart. Here, it doesn't matter whether the crime was committed by a starving child or a deranged adult—the immediate justice system is a mob with sticks."

I folded my arms. "And aren't the police supposed to maintain law and order?"

Alaul let out a dry laugh. "We know better than to interfere. If there's one thing the public hates more than criminals, it's us. We're already stretched thin, and recruitment isn't exactly booming. We're not glorified as "New York's finest" like in those Hollywood shows—if anything, we're branded as "Dhaka's worst." I'd rather not send my men to get beaten into the afterlife."

I shrugged. "Fair enough."

We sat there, waiting for the updated bail order to be faxed from the court. Once it arrived, I filled out the release paperwork—seven extensive forms requiring every possible detail about my life.

Alaul tsked, "You could have saved yourself—and me—a lot of trouble if you had just filled these out and sent them back to me on WhatsApp."

I shot back, "Well, it was a little hard to trust someone who changed their name twice in two days—from Oshim to Alaul."

Alaul sighed, "I thought I was being discreet. Then I realised it was a pointless nuisance—you were going to find out anyway."

As I was filling out the forms, an officer walked in to tell Alaul, "Sir, there's a fellow named Shiro Edwards here, says he's here with the bail money for the Overseer's wife."

I checked my phone and saw international roaming was turned off. Shiro probably couldn't reach me and decided to walk into the station.

Alaul looked at me with a raised eyebrow, silently asking what that was about. I replied, "I arranged for the bail money through other means, just in case..."

Alaul smiled and finished my sentence, "...In case we policemen didn't budge? And didn't anyone also tell you to negotiate bribes instead of paying the 'full' amount?"

I chuckled. "Yes, to both."

Alaul sighed. "We still have a long way to go to earn the public's trust, especially when some in our ranks tarnish the reputation of the rest. Anyway, there's no need for that now. Just finish the release documents here and go spend that bail money on Samira."

A police officer who didn't squirm his way to take money practically sitting on his lap. He was either very honest or had plenty for himself from elsewhere. The latter was rare, as once they start, no one ever has their fill of under-the-table bribery—greed takes over.

After handing in the papers, I stared at Alaul, silently contemplating everything Nida had told me. He let me linger in thought for a moment before snapping me out of it and speaking up, "Well, no point in wasting daylight and keeping your friend waiting. Go take your sister and be gone. Follow me."

I quickly got up to follow Alaul, activating my international roaming once more. Almost immediately, I received an email from the Australian Consulate, confirming they had issued me a replacement photo ID to show at airport immigration on my way out. However, I still had a lot left to handle and wasn't planning to leave anytime soon.

Alaul grabbed the cell keys from the desk officer. As he walked me through the jail corridor to the last cell where Nida was being kept, I noticed Hafiz pressing the screen of a smartphone in the corner of his cell. I paused, and Alaul backtracked to follow my gaze, then screamed at the desk officer, "Who gave '*double standards*' a phone? Take it away right now."

As the desk officer ran to grab the phone, I noticed Hafiz smile at the officer as he surrendered the phone, and silently mouthed, "Thank you." Even when someone does the right thing and follows instructions ethically, their colleague can take over and always undo their efforts with greed or negligence—whichever suits the scene.

Nida was set free, and I motioned for Shiro, who was waiting by the door in t-shirt and jeans, that we were leaving. Nida refused to look at Alaul on her way out.

As Nida walked beside me, she yanked my hand as she used to when we were children. Then she asked, "Kaushal's gone, isn't he?"

I nodded. "Yes."

Tears began to roll down Nida's cheeks, and she silently wept as we made our way toward Shiro's car.

Shiro motioned for me to sit in the back with Nida as I sent him the coordinates for Samira. In the car, Nida grabbed my phone, trying to call Kaushal, clearly in denial. The calls went straight to voicemail. Then, she opened my social media and went straight to Kaushal's profile. She scrolled through the messages on his timeline, her fingers moving rapidly. Most of them were derogatory, mocking him and calling his death "justice served." Though he wasn't the first Overseer of the Turag Project to die, he was by far the most famous, almost a local celebrity. His death had sparked a public outcry, and people were openly laughing, calling it deserved.

After a while, Nida stopped became fixated on a particular post and began to cry. I leaned over to see what she was looking at. Someone had posted a screenshot of Kaushal's confession letter, likely taken from a media outlet. The comments beneath it were filled with laughter and abuse.

The letter read:

"I am Kaushal Veni, now the former Chief Overseer of the Turag Project. I am fully aware of the charges against me: corruption, bribery, and the most unforgivable of all, the sexual assault of actress Pixie Chandan. I confess to every single one of these crimes.

Neither my mother nor my wife, Nida Oman, were aware of my actions. When Nida discovered the truth, she wanted to report me, many times, But I threatened to take our daughter Samira's life if she ever spoke out.

We had several businesses together, but all of that was just a façade. I emotionally blackmailed Nida to put all of her savings into our joint account, planning to take everything from her, to scam her when the time was right. But she got smart and tried to move that money out which frustrated me.

I took out all my frustrations out on her, both physically and emotionally. To ensure she would never speak up, to keep her under my control, I sold her brother, Bashir Oman, to the student league thugs, fully aware of the torture and suffering he would endure. He never chose that path, but I forced him into it, knowing exactly what it would do to him. Nida begged me to bring Bashir back, and I promised her that I would as long as she played along. Bashir had to fight against his own beliefs, and I never intervened. I did not anticipate his death as that stripped me of the leverage I held over Nida.

In the end, Nida fought back. She fought with a knife and called the police. Nida is the real victim in all of this. She never deserved the torment I subjected her to.

This is my final confession. The weight of my actions has become unbearable. I can no longer live with the guilt and pain I've caused. I know Samira will grow up despising me for everything I've done, and I've come to accept that as the only legacy that I will leave her with.

I only hope that the authorities and the media will leave my family in peace. They have already suffered enough. In the end, I couldn't give my family the life that they deserved."

...

Within a day, Kaushal's mother was publicly ridiculed for raising a rapist. Desperate to clear her son's name, she took to the streets, urging anyone who would listen that Kaushal was not the person he had portrayed himself to be. But the weight of the ridicule was too much for her. She eventually withdrew from society, consumed by grief, and passed away quietly in her sleep.

People on social media rarely seek the truth; they only look for validation that they're right. When the news and celebrities align with their speculations, it fuels their confirmation bias, and the official narrative often shifts to cater to that or oppose it entirely, rather than presenting less popular truths that are present somewhere in the middle.

Social media influencers began sharing Nida's story as a symbol of "women's empowerment," treating it as a standard for all women to rise against injustice. They transformed her into a hero, which was likely what Kaushal had hoped for: for Nida and Samira to escape the bad press surrounding the Kaushal Veni Scam. Kaushal's suicide and confession letter sealed the case.

Nida was able to withdraw an enormous sum of money from their joint account, none of which was her contribution. However, Kaushal's confession letter, coupled with the public's overwhelming support for Nida, spared her from any legal scrutiny over the source of the funds. No judge wanted to risk the backlash in a country recently liberated from a dictatorship, where public opinion held considerable sway.

Just as Alaul had predicted, it was a better outcome than the alternative. Some of the more rational social media influencers speculated, that had Kaushal not taken his own life, he would have probably been assassinated anyway for knowing too much about the Turag Project.

In the coming weeks, the opposition party influenced a press release claiming that Kaushal Veni had embezzled almost all of the money that was intended for the Turag Project and made little to no progress beyond laying a few blocks of concrete to create the illusion of progress. As absurd as this announcement sounded, political parties and the local media had fabricated stranger stories in the past—like the one about a group of politically influenced men toppling an eight-story building with their bare hands!

The media hosted elaborate talk shows featuring celebrities who dissected how the now-infamous Kaushal Veni had allegedly laundered vast sums of money, building his entire business empire on wealth stolen from hardworking taxpayers. Meanwhile, more eccentric figures on social media began spinning bizarre tales, claiming the curse of the Turag Project was actually a woman dressed in all white, who had slain Kaushal and forced his ghost to write the confession letter. Both camps had a substantial number of followers, eagerly commenting and sharing the information as if it were fact. It was a stark reminder that when presented in a polished, civilized way, the average person will believe almost anything, as long as enough famous voices back it up. And that's exactly what was happening.

Social media influencers jumped on the 'name-and-shame' bandwagon, recording themselves as they vandalised Kaushal's now-abandoned home, proudly posting it on social media as if they had done a great deed for their country. Only a handful of rational voices saw it for the nonsense it truly was, but quickly lost followers when they spoke out against the belief shared by the masses.

The Turag Project completion date was once again postponed, with a new unveiling date projected fifteen years down the line. Its progress in the last five years was erased, along with the only person who had worked tirelessly against all odds to see it through. Had greed and envy not clouded the judgment of those in power, it might have been completed—transforming millions of lives instead of resuming its role as a longstanding national scam.

Our society loves a story with a tragic hero or a well-crafted villain without considering that no one is perfect. There is a villain in all of us, just as much as there is a hero. The public conveniently forgot Nida's family ties to Beebo for which they once unfairly sent her horrible threats, and instead now cast her as the tragic hero—someone who fought back against her corrupt, monstrous husband. As expected, the media and celebrities painted Kaushal as a well-crafted villain because that was what those in power decided Kaushal should be, manipulating the narrative just enough to overlook his qualities and emphasise only on his flaws.

And that was how the story played out. Soon, videos of a woman stuffing noodles into a cooked chicken went viral, and both the media and public lost interest in the Turag Project Scandal, completely forgetting about Kaushal Veni. Because, of course, why would the media cover a story of how Nida spent days kneeling in front of Kaushal's grave—the one she spent a fortune securing next to our father's—with an empty grave in between, likely reserved for herself?

On Kaushal's death anniversary, Nida was invited for a talk show interview titled "*How Kaushal Veni scammed a bleeding heart*". Despite my urging her not to go through with it, she agreed. While the interviewer highlighted all of Kaushal's flaws, she spoke only of his good qualities—because, as our mother always taught us, if you can't say something good about someone, don't say anything at all. Naturally, that interview was not aired, and she was never invited back. When it's easier to please a crowd by validating their beliefs, why bother representing *unpopular opinions*?

Also by Taseef Farook

Unpopular Opinions Book Series
Unpopular Opinions
Unpopular Opinions 2
Troubled Waters
Scam a Bleeding Heart

www.ingramcontent.com/pod-product-compliance
Lightning Source LLC
Chambersburg PA
CBHW022024170626
46808CB00003B/1054